Sometimes I think I'm crazy. Not going crazy. Already there. Instead of sleep, I wrestle with vague ideas of who he is, or rather, who I thought he was. Or maybe just who I wanted him to be. I reach for the phone when I remember the definition of insanity…doing the same thing over and over again and expecting different results.

Only crazy people can't let go.

THE
CHARLIE DIAZ
SYNDROME

A WORK OF FICTION

MICHELLE GARCIA

ISBN: 0615703739

ISBN 13: 9780615703732

"I'm fine. The apartment's great. Stop worrying." I paced around the stylish, fully-furnished apartment in track pants and a tank top, "I'm already unpacked."

"Well, all you had were your clothes. I can't believe you got rid of all of your stuff."

"New city, new stuff."

"I still think you should've come here with us," she sighed.

"Oh, you. Just stop. I'll be up for the premier party. And the wrap party. And any other party you can get me invited to."

I laughed – she didn't.

It was only seven weeks earlier when my boss and good friend, Dee Dee Donovan, told me she was closing 3D Talent Management and moving to New York City. Her son had finally made it in the acting game after a decade of commercials and most notably, as the face of the United Negro College Fund. With filming of the primetime drama done mostly on-location in NYC, he had to move and as manager and mother of the 20 year old neophyte, she was going with him.

"I'll start making some calls, everyone needs a good assistant and you're the best. You do it all," she started rattling off the names of other agents we knew that might need someone, jotting notes on the blotter in the center of her desk. She sat stunned in the overstuffed executive chair behind her big oak desk as I explained that I wouldn't be staying in L.A.

I was excited when she invited me to move with her and the company to Los Angeles to be closer to opportunities for Derrick's career. And although I welcomed the idea of not having to endure Chicago winters, I found it difficult to fit into the Hollywood scene.

I would be furious when people asked me what agency I was with – as though every woman of a certain age living in L.A. must be pursuing a career in show business. Can't a secretary – or *personal assistant*, just be that? Why was everything a competition?

Los Angeles became very bad for my ego when I realized to be noticed you had to be tall, blonde and a 44D created by *"Doctor du Jour"*. I had a nice figure but nothing like the amazons that stroll L.A. by day as waitresses and troll Hollywood clubs by night looking to make the right connections.

I remember one time Derrick insisted I go with him to the cast party for some teen drama show. What a mistake. I never felt so old, fat and uncool in my entire life. It was enough that I wasn't an actress and didn't want to be one but when I stumbled upon a group of tiny teenage girls and a cocaine streaked mirror I knew it was time to go.

There was no way I'd stay in L.A. without Dee and Derrick.

"I had no idea you were so unhappy," she said as she dried the tears that escaped her dark eyes.

"I'm happy. I've been very happy here. But there's no reason for me to be in L.A. if you're not here."

After 15 minutes of her insisting I move to New York, she finally understood. She had to let me go and I had to do the same.

"You're like a sister to me," she smiled and blotted more tears from her cheeks.

She was right, if not so much for her part, certainly for mine. Estranged from my family, she and Derrick were the closest thing I had to family in a long time. And while I spent most of the major holidays holed up in my apartment with baked ziti and John Hughes' movies, I did occasionally spend a holiday with Dee and her extended family.

Our bond grew not only from working together but from her unfaltering loyalty. She stood by me during all of the chaos with Jeff Syddall and never judged me. I knew I could count on her honesty and wisdom. She didn't condemn me for making mistakes but showed me how to make better decisions and I loved her for it.

"It's not an easy decision but it's the right one," I smiled at her and tried not to let the doubt show on my face.

"Bianca, you're probably the strongest person I know. You just don't even know how goddamn much I admire you."

"Thank you."

"So, what will you do? Go back to Chicago?"

"No!" I snapped in an inadvertently punitive tone. I shifted in my seat and rephrased, "I mean, no. I'm not going back to Chicago."

"Well," she counted on her fingers, "if you don't stay here, and you don't come to New York, and you don't go back to Chicago, where you gonna go?"

Having vacationed with her in Washington D.C. that spring, it was my first and only choice.

Diane, Dee's sister, was the older of the two women and was a frequent visitor both in Chicago and Los Angeles. She lived in D.C. where her husband was a cardiologist to politicos and foreign dignitaries. Her very beautiful home in Potomac, Maryland was the closest thing to a mansion I'd ever seen. I had gotten to know Diane and her husband, Corbin, over the years and I learned "new money" isn't always ugly.

When I told Dee Dee I was thinking about moving to D.C. she did what she could to talk me out of it.

"It's just so political," she sighed.

Although it seemed she wasn't, I was impressed with all of the nice people we'd met during our visits with Diane. And with Dee only a short train ride away in New York City, it seemed ideal. When she realized I was serious, she called Diane and asked if she could help me. I begged her to not bother her sister but she insisted.

"She can do it and you deserve it. Consider it part of a severance package," she thrust a set of keys into my palm a few weeks later. "It's not forever but it should give you enough time to find a place."

I hugged her neck and thanked her again.

She refused to let me go, "Please just be careful." We stood there hugging for a long moment until she finally released me from her embrace. She touched my face and smiled, tears streaked down her cheeks, "You come see us any time you want."

I nodded and we hugged again. I quickly turned and left the now empty office where I'd worked the last four years.

I remember the feeling I had when I left L.A. in my modest sedan and headed east on the I-10, *"How many times will I regret this decision?"*

But now standing in the studio apartment I wasn't regretting a thing. Dee and I stayed on the phone talking for a while, mostly about Derrick's hectic shooting schedule and how tiny her upper West Side apartment was.

Her last question before we hung up, "When are you coming for a visit?"

"Soon. I promise."

I didn't expect to become a regular at the bar inside the Westin, it just sort of happened. Our company often put people up at this particular hotel because it was close to our office. Sometimes out-of-town guests, other times people from my office, sleeping in shifts while working on a particularly urgent project. Often working well after midnight, it was easier and sometimes safer to rest there for a few hours rather than drive all the way home. I decided to stop in one afternoon when the 12-lane highway I used to get to and from work was backed up by a Presidential motorcade.

The quiet, anonymous atmosphere of the bar was a perfect setting for a relaxing cocktail after a long day. The décor was sleek and dark, a stark contrast to the bright, open feel of the lobby. There was music playing from an unmanned DJ booth and as I rounded the u-shaped bar, I found stairs leading down to a dance floor with a bank of pool tables on the far side. The 30-something bartender smiled pleasantly and I could barely see the hint of a tongue stud as she asked me what I'd like to drink.

"Surprise me," I smiled at her and put a ten dollar bill on the bar in front of me.

She asked if I worked in the area or if I was a guest at the hotel.

"I work down the street," I sipped the very strong cranberry and vodka concoction. "This is just a delaying tactic. I heard there was a lot of traffic."

"So you're new to town?" She smiled at a man who'd just walked in from the side door and sat down on the far side of the bar.

"What makes you ask?"

"There's always traffic in this town," she smiled and took the money, putting an empty upside-down shot glass in front of me. She began pouring a draft beer and without saying a word handed it to the man who'd just sat down. He was an older gentleman, maybe late 50's.

He asked the bartender in a husky, smoker's voice, "Hey, Brandi, who's that?"

"I don't know," she turned to face me. "She just walked in a minute before you got here."

"Hey, darling, what's your name?" He called out.

Just as I was about to answer, a familiar face walked in the door behind the friendly stranger.

"What are you doing here?" He was smiling as he strode over to meet me and surprised me with a hug instead of a handshake.

Greg Schicker was friends with Diane's husband and I'd met him a few times during previous visits with Dee Dee. He was very tall, with guy-next-door good looks and a slender but solid build. He was cerebral and witty, a talker, that always seemed "on". Even when discussing the most mundane things, I would think to myself, "*allegedly*".

He took a seat next to me, resting his left arm on the bar and right foot on the bottom of my bar stool as I explained why I'd moved and where I was living. Every few minutes Greg would look over his shoulder to the stranger drinking his beer on the opposite side of the bar. He'd smile and wink each time before returning his attention back to me. Within half-hour or so a group of six or seven people walked in together and the bar began to fill from the original handful of people when I arrived.

"Hey, Schicker," one of the men said as he patted Greg's back, throwing an engaging glance at me on his way to join their friends at a booth nearby.

"Bring your friend over here," another hollered over the music.

"Do you wanna join us?" All 6'4" of him stood up and towered over me. He held out a long arm to show the way.

"I wasn't really planning on being here much longer," I said as I contemplated the offer.

"Really?" He reached around me and picked up the upside down shot glass, apparently a sign I had a drink credit. With a smile that was a perfect match for his all-American looks he insisted, "Come on, come meet some nice people." He put his arm around my shoulders and walked me over to the corner booth near the now manned DJ booth.

Most of the people at the table were Tyson McCullough's co-workers from the Legal Department of the large engineering contractor where Greg also worked. Greg was an Optical Engineer with special emphasis on the advanced application of light and told me because of the nature of his work, primarily with the U.S. Department of Defense, he couldn't really talk about it.

Ty eventually asked me what I did for a living.

"I support the Directors of Radiological Assessment and Emergency Preparedness so nuclear power plants can maintain their license from the NRC. Really, I'm a secretary."

"Well, that's cool," Elizabeth said. "I'm a secretary too and trust me, I think I know more about the law than Ty does," she laughed and playfully swatted his arm.

"I really like it and I work with a lot of interesting people."

"Hey, girl, if you like your job and you get paid your fair share, that's all good." She raised her glass, "To the men in charge and the women who know what's going on."

I nursed my drink as they chatted on about work, mutual friends and an upcoming card party.

"You should come," Elizabeth said as she took a sip of her very expensive brandy.

I smiled at her suggestion.

"I'll bring her with me," Greg winked at her and spun around to the bar behind him to get another round of drinks.

It wasn't long until I was in the routine of Thursday and Friday evenings at the Westin. I was glad to have somewhere to be other than at home alone. Alone with memories and regrets that haunted me. Thoughts of Jeff Syddall still trapped in my mind making my head spin even all these years later.

Most of the time I just listened as everyone talked about something funny that happened at work or something related to football and the on-going debate on how unfair the Redskins' schedule would be. A couple of times I took Greg up on his offer to shoot pool only to find I wasn't that bad of a shot. And sometimes the DJ would play an irresistibly danceable song and we ladies were happy to oblige.

One weekend Lynn, the Office Manager and only other administrative person in my office, and I had to share a room at the Westin while working on a particularly enormous proposal for a large West Coast client. Just after midnight Saturday when we finally finished the proposal, we decided to stay the night instead of driving home after working almost 60 hours in three days.

We were fully-clothed in far more casual than usual office attire on our respective beds when I suddenly felt energized. I wondered if Greg and the others were downstairs at the bar.

"I sometimes meet up with friends at the hotel bar. It's pretty nice," I paused waiting for an immediate rejection. "You wanna head down for a drink?"

Lynn sat up slowly, her hair messy and clothes disheveled, "Hell yeah." She had a sudden gleam in her eyes.

As we exited the elevator, I heard music coming from the direction of the bar. The place was full and loud, thick with heat. I saw Lynn smile as we walked in, "This is my song," she yelled over the noise of the crowd and music. We twisted through the mob of people and made our way to the bar. Lynn took out a twenty and held her hand straight out, waiting to get the attention of one of the four bartenders that were working. She ordered two identical drinks and handed me one. I took a tentative sip.

"Vodka tonic," she said loud enough for me to hear. "Let's go down to the dance floor, it looks like there may be a spot down there," she pointed down the stairs to my right. We took our drinks and found a vacant bar stool high table located on the perimeter of the dance floor. We stood on opposite sides, looking around and watching the various activities. Some people dancing, some shooting pool, others throwing darts and of course, the crowd at the bar upstairs.

"I like this place," she shouted over the music.

"Me, too. My friends and I come here on Thursdays, sometimes Fridays." I knew full-well it was a much more routine thing but didn't know how it might sound.

She nodded her head to the music, "Let me know next time and I'll meet you up here."

"OK." I yelled hoping she could hear me over the almost deafening music.

We finished our drinks in a quick way and I was headed to get another round when I felt a tap on the shoulder. I turned around and found Ty holding an empty beer mug.

"I thought that was you," he smiled and hugged me.

"Hey, Ty. Is everyone else here?"

"No, I'm here with some clients from Brazil." Pointing over his shoulder I saw a group of well-dressed men with white oxford shirt sleeves rolled up and loosened ties huddled around the line of tape on the floor in front of one of the dart boards.

"Brazil?" Lynn drew Ty's attention to her, "I've heard Bianca speaking Portuguese, it's a beautiful language. Are you fluent?"

He shook his head and smiled, "Not a word." He put down his empty mug and reached out to shake her hand, "Bianca, be so kind as to introduce me to your friend."

"Lynn, this is Ty. Ty, that's Lynn. We work together." I hoped this information would keep him from contradicting my previous statement to her about the frequency of my visits to this particular establishment.

"Nice to meet you, Lynn," he continued smiling and lingered in their handshake.

From then on, Lynn became part of our group of regulars.

* * *

When I first started at the satellite office of the large nuclear consulting firm I was a little anxious. Not just because of Lynn's tenure with the company and the fact that she'd previously been the only admin in the office but because the people I worked for and with, all Ph.D's or ex-U.S. Navy nuclear engineers, were brilliant, well-known and highly respected in their field. It was sometimes a challenge to keep up and there had definitely been a learning curve since I'd come from a completely different industry. I had useful skills, typing almost 100 words per minute, working knowledge of over 30 different software packages and speaking three languages fluently but the very things that made me confident I could do my job were the same things that seemed to intimidate her.

Lynn Weaver was in her early 40's, a single mother of two teenage boys. Her ex-husband was a former site-assigned engineer for the company and when they divorced, she stayed in contact with the Vice President, then Director of Site Assignments for Eastern Operations.

After she lost her job at a large telecom firm, she was offered the job of sole office support and had been there ever since. I think it was a difficult pill for her to swallow as she didn't even interview me. It was almost like, "You want her, you hire her." Shortly after I started with the company, she had to take a leave of absence and it gave me a chance to prove that even though I was almost 20 years her junior, I was professional and able to handle the responsibility. She reminded me so much of my dear friend and former boss, Dee Dee, that I couldn't help but feel an affinity for her even if she didn't immediately feel one for me.

My self-appointed mentor was Tommy Payton, a 47 year old Stanford graduate and wildly charismatic man. He was the kind of man that even other men loved to be around. As the most prolific of all the scientists in the office, I tried to keep my mouth shut and learn as much as I could from him. But after catching an error he made – a particularly close call on a "dress drill" – he said I deserved a raise for not only catching the error but having the nerve to point it out. A few days later, I heard him start a conversation with our boss, "You can't expect this woman to live on the pittance you're paying her..." then closing the door to have a private conversation with the VP. He never told me what was said or what made him think I was underpaid but the following payday I calculated an incredible twenty percent raise. Tommy smiled as he walked by the morning of the first paycheck with the increase, knocked his big college class ring on the corner of my desk and with a wink said, "Lunch is on you today, kid."

As the clock ticked down on my lovely but very expensive apartment, the raise bought me some much needed time to start getting serious about looking for a place.

"Charlie's a good guy, comes here once in a blue moon or so."
Charlie Diaz had arrived almost two hours after the rest of our little group had gotten there. He nodded, barely looking at me or acknowledging what Greg said. He seemed distracted and more interested in getting downstairs to the bank of pool tables. A short while later, as some of the usual group started to leave, I thought I'd go down and say good bye. As I approached the stairs, Greg came bounding up and asked if I wanted to stay and shoot some pool.

"No way, don't waste your money. I suck."

"I know. You're Diaz's partner," he said hurriedly.

I felt myself immediately blush and my heart start to pound in my chest. Why would Charlie want me as his partner? He hadn't said a word, not even "hello" when Greg introduced us but only half-nodded and avoided eye contact.

"Ty and me, against you and Charlie," Greg smiled and motioned with his head toward the pool tables behind him.

There stood Charlie, drinking a draft beer and watching Ty rack. When he turned to my direction, I quickly looked away.

Why all the intimidation? I couldn't understand it. At 5'6" and wearing 2-1/2" heels, I was almost as tall as he was. I was stylishly dressed, like any other woman in the bar but insecurity nagged at me and told me a man as handsome as Charlie was just a little out of reach.

"Well?" Greg prodded, "You gonna play or stand there staring at the door?"

I turned back to Greg, "Did you tell him how bad I am at this? Are you guys playing for money? Am I a ringer?"

"A ringer would mean you're good," he scoffed. "Anyway, it wasn't my idea, it was Charlie's."

Mr. Hugo Boss with the very expensive, double Italian silk tie, what was he thinking?

"Just c'mon and play," he playfully nudged me with his shoulder.

My heart leapt and I drew a deep breath, "I guess I shouldn't let him down, huh?"

"Most women wouldn't," Greg said with a half-hearted smile.

I felt self-conscious as I walked down the stairs and crossed the dance floor to the pool tables.

"Hey, look who's gonna shoot pool with us," Ty said with a smile.

I smiled and looked directly at Charlie, "I hope you know what you're getting yourself into."

He leaned his body across the pool table and lined up his break shot, "Likewise."

He wasn't kidding.

"What are you doing this weekend? You think you wanna help me look for a place to live?" I tried not to sound as pathetic as I felt.

"You'll find something, don't worry," Lynn said in a calm voice as traffic screamed in the background.

"Where are you?"

"Oh, I'm out here trying to get my car in for service," now she sounded annoyed.

"Let me let you go, we'll just talk at work."

"We're fine. I can talk," I heard the sound of a car horn.

"I know I'm just slightly freaking out. I want – "

My other line interrupted us. I had no way to know who it was but I knew who I hoped it would be.

"Hey, Lynn, I gotta take this other call."

"Tell me it's Charlie," she screeched.

"I don't know, I'll call you back," I said impatiently.

"If you don't call me back, I'll know it's him," she laughed and hung up.

I quickly pressed the button and heard the phone click to the incoming call on the other line. "Hello, it's Bianca," I was trying to sound calm even though it felt like my heart was going to jump out of my chest.

"Hi, Charlie Diaz here."

I squeezed my eyes shut and pounded my fist on the sofa cushion next to me. "Hi," I tried to mask my giddiness.

"What are you doing right now?" He asked in his breathy voice.

"I was talking to Lynn, sitting here thinking about things."

"About me?" He asked in an irresistibly sexy way.

"How did you know?" I sounded as flirtatious as I could.

He laughed, "I just wanted to call and check on you."

"I'm very well, thank you. How are you?"

"Good," he answered quickly and then silence hung in the air.

"OK. Well, enjoy the rest of your weekend," I said, expecting to hang up since neither of us was saying anything.

"So, you don't want to talk to me the rest of the weekend?"

"I wasn't. Umm. I didn't mean it that way." I exhaled quietly and started again, "I thought you were trying to finish the conversation and hang up. So I was just moving in that direction."

"Relax."

I broke into nervous laughter, "I'll try. I just have a lot on my mind."

"Like what?"

"Well, I don't know if I mentioned it but I only have another few weeks in this apartment. After that, I have to figure out if I can swing the rent or move into the slums of Gaithersburg."

"I'm not doing anything tomorrow. I can take you around, show you some places."

Charlie offering to help me find a place to live? I had to force myself to calm down. "I would love that," I tightened my voice and tried to hide my enthusiasm.

"OK. I'll pick you up in the morning."

"That's great – " and before we could nail down any details, the line went dead. I figured he'd call back but he didn't. I wasn't sure what to think. I didn't know if he knew where I lived or what time he planned to come over. All I knew was he'd offered to take me out and I was giddy like a schoolgirl at the thought of seeing him again.

I could hardly sleep that night. As I flipped through the Apartment Finder Guide and *The Gazette*, I tried to map out an efficient route through the various desirable suburbs and properties I wanted to see, wondering if I'd be seeing them with him by my side.

But at the forefront of my mind was the previous evening, the night I first met Charlie Diaz.

* * *

I remember Greg asking me to play pool and as the evening went on, Charlie and I got closer. He would gently hug me after every made shot and sometimes after missed ones. I recalled the warmth of his body, the smell of his cologne and feeling like I could melt from the combination.

The dim light shone in Charlie's hazel green eyes, making them seem darker and more intense than earlier in the evening or perhaps I was only just noticing because I was finally getting the courage to look him in the eyes. He would huddle close to me explaining the geometry and "leaves" as Greg and Ty made their shots. I already understood the basic geometrical principals and logic of the set up but I let him explain. I didn't know if he was trying to make me a better pool player or just trying to be close to me.

I didn't care.

We finished our second game and headed back up to the bar when I decided to call it an evening. I'd had three vodka tonics in two hours and felt a high from the mixture of flirtation and sexual chemistry. I needed to escape while I could.

After saying good night to the rest of the group and then specifically to Charlie, I headed out the side door to the parking lot. I could hear the music swell behind me, as someone was following me but I refused to turn around. I already had an idea who it was.

I was only six or seven steps ahead of him but Charlie did not quicken his pace or call out to me. When I reached my car, he walked up behind me and kept me from opening the door so I turned to face him, "Let me take you home," he said.

My knees went weak and I smiled, "Why?" I asked, trying hard not to kiss him.

"I'd feel better if you let me take you home," he cocked his head to the side, "I just wanna know you're safe."

"What if I told you that I'll be fine?" The urge to kiss him was starting to get the better of me.

He smiled and inched closer, "Can I at least give you a kiss?"

I felt the one corner of my mouth go up, "Where?" I gave him a coy smile.

As I was leaned up against the car, he put one hand low on my hip, the other moved to my neck so his thumb was directly under my ear. He kissed my cheek, "Good night, Bianca. Be good." He brushed his lips past mine on the way to kissing my other cheek. He then spun around and walked briskly back to the door we'd just exited. I could see a tall figure watching us but I didn't know who it was. I exhaled and looked around the parking lot to see if anyone else was taking in the view.

Lying on my bed with this memory, I started to run my fingers through my shoulder-length hair, wondering how it would feel to run my fingers through his thick, dark hair.

I hadn't had a real relationship with anyone since Jeff Syddall. I figured maybe I was finally ready. I was smarter now. Older. The thing with Jeff had left scars emotionally and physically but in so many ways he made me a better person.

Stronger.

Jeff taught me people can say a lot of things but it's what they do that makes them who they really are.

Charlie could be exactly what I need. He felt so good fully-clothed, I fantasized about how he must feel skin-on-skin. I bargained with myself how long I'd wait before bedding him.

"Yes, I would like to fuck Charlie Diaz," I thought as I drifted off to sleep.

* * *

I awoke suddenly to a firm knock at the door. Startled, I turned to the alarm clock that read 8:14 AM.

"Hold on a minute," I jumped out of bed, my heart pounded in my chest with anxiety. "Who is it?" I called as I approached the door and peered through the peephole.

Through the small fish-eye view, I could see Charlie standing there with his back to the door. Sleep mingled with nervousness as I contemplated opening the door in just panties and a t-shirt. Even in my state of sleep and undress, I proudly swung the door open and invited him in.

As he turned around to accept my invitation, I saw he had a cup of coffee in each hand. He was smiling and about to say something until he noticed what I was wearing or actually not wearing.

"I know it's early," he apologized as he walked in.

"I'm sorry. I'm not ready. I didn't know what time you'd be here. Our call got cut off."

He walked over to the breakfast bar and put down the two cups of coffee.

"I'll just be a minute."

He reached for me as I walked by, pulled me close to him and began kissing me. His mouth was warm and skilled as he worked mine. His arms wrapped around me and he began to walk me backward to the bed. I couldn't believe what was happening. I hadn't even brushed my teeth.

We kissed passionately, then stared at each other as he hurriedly kicked off his shoes and pulled his Polo shirt up over his head and let it fall to the floor. We resumed kissing and fell onto the bed. He stroked my hair, "God you're beautiful," he sighed and put his mouth back on mine.

I wanted to swallow him. I wanted him to swallow me. Our kissing turned into playful biting and then back to deep, passionate kissing. I felt so comfortable, so in sync with him. I opened my eyes to find him watching me. I smiled at him, held him tighter and wrapped one leg around one of his. His sexy confidence was encouraging my own. We rolled over so that I could be on top. He held my face and controlled our kissing for several minutes. I wanted to reach for his jeans but I couldn't work up the courage. How could I be doing this so soon? I met him barely 36 hours earlier.

"You're so beautiful," he said again, and kissed me feverishly. "You're so fucking sexy," he held me tight and pulled me closer to his hardness. I could feel my own arousal building. I pulled back and looked at him. His eyes were a bright and wide open. He smiled, "How are you this morning?"

"I'm very fine this morning," I smiled back at him.

Still smiling he asked, "So you wanna go look for a place?"

I couldn't believe what I was hearing. Did he really want to leave our current situation? "Ummm. Yeah." I was suddenly embarrassed by my arousal, "I mean, yes."

"What's wrong, Bianca?" His lips saying my name touched me in a familiar place.

"Nothing," I started to roll off of him but he didn't let go.

"What – is – wrong?" He held me in my place on top of him.

"Seriously, nothing," I stayed in his arms and resisted the urge to wriggle away.

"You're mad I don't wanna fuck you right now?" His choice of words was surprising but his tone was not unpleasant.

"No," I snapped quickly. "It's not that. I just wasn't ready for you, I mean, I didn't know what time to expect you so I didn't straighten up or take a shower or anything yet."

He let go and gently rolled me off of him. He sat up as I did, and looked back to me. "I'm sorry I didn't call you back. I got busy and I've lost my damn phone. So, I thought I'd surprise you with coffee."

"You did surprise me," I scuttled to the bathroom and put on my bathrobe.

"I surprised myself if you really wanna know," he said with a sigh. "I didn't mean to come on so strong. I was just – " he stopped.

I walked out of the bathroom in my kimono style robe over my shirt, "Just what?"

"Nothing. I had an urge to kiss you, so I did. Want some coffee?" He got off the bed and reached for the coffees on the breakfast bar.

"Excellent," I said and joined him near the kitchenette. He handed me the warm cup and I took a careful sip.

Charlie noticed the clippings and apartment listings on the bar, "You have an agenda, huh?" He slurped the hot liquid from his cup.

"Absolutely. I'm a planner."

* * *

Charlie waited while I quickly took a shower and got ready to go apartment hunting. I wasn't one to fuss much with hair or makeup anyway but I wanted to make sure I didn't look like a total slob, especially compared to someone as impeccably dressed as Mr. Diaz. Even though I didn't wash my hair, it didn't look dirty but looked more like a tousled mess, as if it was supposed to look that way.

"You look nice," he smiled at me as we walked to his car. There was something so genuine in his tone and I absolutely believed he meant what he said even if I knew different.

We drove to the opposite side of the Capital Beltway. "I hope you don't mind. I wanted to show you some places in PG. It's probably as close to your office as anywhere else," he briefly looked over at me.

"Sure," I smiled and watched the highway fly by us.

We arrived to a brick, six-flat in a single family home neighborhood.

"This is nice," he said getting out of the car.

"This neighborhood is incredible. How much is the rent?" I looked around admiring the lush landscaping on the tree lined street.

"I don't know," he said and came around to where I stood to escort me to the building.

We looked at several apartments in the same style. Lots of brownstone apartment buildings oddly situated in old, established neighborhoods. It was almost noon before Charlie asked if I wanted to get headed back to the other side of the Beltway.

"Sure. Let's hit this one place I heard about off of Shady Grove and then I'll buy you lunch."

He nodded his head, "Deal."

As the leasing agent walked us through the display unit, Charlie walked behind me holding my shoulders, "This is nice. Different than what we looked at this morning."

"So, will it be just the two of you?"

"No," I laughed a nervous laugh, "it's just me."

He let go of me as we entered the master bedroom area.

"And, what do you do Miss?"

"You can call me Bianca."

"Bianca," the prematurely gray woman repeated, "what do you do for a living?"

She and Charlie both listened intently as I explained an overview of what my company did and the small role I played in making it happen. Charlie was once again behind me, now holding my hands as I talked. I could feel him pleasantly violating my personal space.

"Can you give us a minute to talk?" He asked the woman.

"Sure, I'll leave the key and you can bring it back to the office."

"Of course," he smiled as the woman left.

Just as soon as the door closed, he turned to me, "Did you see the size of the bathroom?" He grabbed my hand and led the way.

I started to make observations about the ample storage space when he hushed me. He turned me to face the mirror as he put his arms around me. His hands inspected my breasts and stomach as we stared at our reflection in the mirror. "Look at you," he was firm in his tone. His hands worked up to my neck and tilted my head, "You're really something, you know that?" He breathed in my ear and gently kissed my neck.

I closed my eyes and sighed as he moved his hands down my stomach over my jeans and alternately slid one hand then the other between my legs. I let my head fall back and rest on his shoulder as he breathed in my ear and said he wanted me. His lips tickled my ear as he planted butterfly kisses on my earlobe. He suddenly stopped and turned me to face him. I could feel his erection through his jeans as he pulled me close, "So, where did you wanna go for lunch?"

* * *

Over our very long lunch Charlie told me more about himself. He was originally from Cleveland, Ohio and had moved to D.C. permanently after graduating from Georgetown. He was 34, an only child, never married and an avid runner. He explained that he was doing fine with his current position but wanted to move on to something new.

"So, now you know about me, let's hear about you."

I smiled and drew a deep breath, "I actually quite like hearing about you."

"Ah, well, I'd like to hear about you for a while," he finished his ice-water, chewing on the last bits of ice that had slid into his mouth.

I immediately presented the sanitized version of my life where the mess with Jeff Sydall didn't exist.

"Bianca, this isn't a job interview," he motioned to our waitress and asked for more water. "You want something?"

I waved him off.

I liked him. I wanted him to like me. But how could I explain everything? Where I come from, why I'm here. He was so honest and didn't mind telling me all about his life, about being raised in Ohio, a close relationship with his grandmother, 2nd generation American-born Spaniard.

"Well, let's start easy. Where did you go to school?"

Could I really tell him?

"OK, how about where you're from? No one is *from* D.C." he said with a wink.

I talked about Dee Dee and her exceptional trust of me, giving me a great job when I was so young. I told him about the time I'd spent in L.A. with my last job but I avoided talking about anything too personal.

"And what brought you to D.C.?"

"Well, some things changed with the business and Dee Dee had to refocus. When she closed the company, I found myself out of a job and figured there was no reason to stay in California. I'd just come from a visit here and have always enjoyed D.C."

"Where's your family?"

I danced around the subject as long as I could and then simply asked, "Can we talk about something else?"

"Sure," he smiled and made a gesture with one hand as if to say 'go ahead'.

"What kind of sports do you like?" This was a subject I loved and hoped we could talk about. Thankfully, he obliged. We talked about the Chicago Bears and how much I loved football. "And I really love March Madness," I said with a smile and finished the last bite of my chicken.

"You like college hoops?" He looked surprised.

"Well, I don't know so much that I like college ball but I love the whole bracketology thing and how anything can happen. It's kinda my religion. I never work the first two days of the NCAA Tournament," I giggled and took a small bite of one of my French fries.

My excitement seemed to charm him. "I'm not usually a college ball fan either but I watch during March Madness. I like how it exposes parity and gives a stage to smaller schools with great programs that might not otherwise get on national TV. To March Madness," he looked at me over his glass and made a toasting gesture, "we found something we both like."

We sat in silence for several minutes when Charlie suddenly reached over and put his hand on mine, "Do you wanna go soon?"

It took everything I had to keep from shouting, "Yes!" I simply smiled and nodded. He looked at me for a long moment then motioned for the waitress to bring our check.

"I'll be right back," I said as we waited for the bill.

"Sure," he said and stood up as I left.

I grinned from ear-to-ear as I walked to the ladies' room. As I washed my hands, I thought about the intense makeout session earlier in the day. Just as I started to get aroused again, I broke from my memories so I could rejoin my very handsome, very charming date.

As I turned the corner, I saw a woman sitting in my seat. She noticed me approaching but didn't move and said nothing when I got to the table.

"Take care," he called over his shoulder as we walked away from the very attractive brunette still sitting there.

"I paid the check," was all he said as he put his arm on my back and led me to the car. I wondered who the woman was but didn't ask and by the time we got to the car, it was obvious he wasn't going to voluntarily tell me.

I was so annoyed that I'd completely forgotten that I was supposed to be buying him lunch as a thank-you for chauffeuring me around all day. We drove back to my apartment with only chit-chat about the food and the atmosphere. When we arrived, to my surprise, he parked and got out of the car. As we walked to the building, I had the urge to ask him who the hell the bitch from the restaurant was, but I didn't want my jealousy to show. I thought maybe I'd ask casually, "So why didn't you introduce me to your friend?" But I said nothing as we rode the elevator to my 5th floor apartment.

"So, why don't you ask me?" He said as we got off the elevator.

"Ask you what?"

"You wanna know who that woman was, don't you?"

"Actually, no. If you don't wanna tell me," I couldn't hide the irritation in my tone. "Lord knows there are things I don't plan on telling you."

"Don't be that way," he said as I unlocked the door and showed him in. I immediately headed to the kitchen to pour myself a glass of sparkling water. He took the glass from my hand and set it on the counter, then put my arms his waist, "I don't know who she is. When you left the table, she came over and introduced herself."

"And sat down," I lightly struggled and got my hands free from his. "May I get you anything?"

"No. But I do want you to look at me," he turned his back to the counter and leaned against it. "I didn't introduce you because it wasn't necessary. I don't know her."

"It was just weird to see another woman sitting there. I was only gone a few minutes."

He pulled me to him, "I'm here with you. I wanna be here with you. You can't be jealous of other women, Bianca. It's not healthy."

I was insulted but knew he was right. I was jealous. Very jealous.

"Look, it's been a long day – "

Charlie interrupted, "You want me to leave?"

"Would you be upset if I said yes?" I pulled away from him and walked around to the breakfast bar side of the kitchen.

"Upset? No. Surprised." He followed me out of the kitchen and went over to the sofa. He sat casually on the arm and looked at me, "Is that what you want?"

"What I really want is a shower."

"The question is, do you want me to go?" He lightly licked his bottom lip and waited for my answer.

Everything told me it was time for him to go. My good sense said I needed to ask him to leave.

"No," I was surprised at my honesty. The truth was, I wanted him there. "Will you wait for me while I take a quick shower?"

He exhaled heavily and smiled, "As long as you want me here, I can be here."

"Even though it's Sunday?"

"I don't have a curfew," he said with a wry smile. "Just go take your shower. I'll be right here," he smiled and slid into the cushions of the large sectional sofa.

"I'll do that, meanwhile, make yourself at home. Watch TV or use the laptop over there," I waved toward the kitchen where the laptop sat on the counter, "whatever you wanna do."

"Whatever?" He asked with a sexy raise of one eyebrow.

"I'll be out in ten minutes," I giggled and headed for the bathroom. I showered quickly, not wanting to miss any time with him. I put on a white t-shirt and black shorts. I had just begun to blow dry my hair when I heard a knock at the door. I quickly turned off the hair dryer and swung the door open.

"May I use the bathroom?"

"I'm so sorry – of course." I unplugged the appliance and hung it on the small hook next to the towel rack. As I started to leave, he stopped me with an outstretched hand to my neck and pulled me to him for a kiss. I was happy to feel his mouth again. I wrapped my arms around him, reaching up his back and pulling him to me. My mouth ravenous on his, I pushed my tongue into his mouth and kissed him.

"OK, OK," he said with a laugh and gently pushing me away, "I'll be out in a minute." I slowly slid my arms from around him as he turned to close the door.

A few minutes later, I heard the shower. "What is he doing?" I asked aloud and laughed, "He doesn't have any clothes here." I shook my head and made my way down the short hall into the main part of the apartment. I noticed the bed was now made and newly washed dishes drying in the dish rack.

The smile on my face grew to an ear-to-ear grin, "Is this guy real?" I put my hand over my mouth and tried not to squeal. I reprimanded myself for such an overreaction. "He didn't build the Great Wall, he made the fucking bed."

The shower went silent and Charlie walked out of the bathroom wearing only navy blue boxer shorts. His dark hair looked even darker wet, in his hands he was holding his neatly-folded clothes.

"That felt great," he announced, "you have great water pressure here." He put his clothes on a stool at the breakfast bar and walked over to me.

"You can get back to drying your hair or whatever," he kissed my forehead as he reached the sofa where I sat channel surfing.

"I hope you don't mind, I took a shower."

"Not at all." I took my now empty glass to the kitchen, "I meant it, make yourself at home. Although, I didn't mean for you to clean. That wasn't necessary but thank you." I gave him a grateful smile as I washed my glass.

"Come here." He took my hand and pulled me to him, "Will you leave the door open while you dry your hair?" He brushed my still damp hair away from my face.

I didn't say anything but did as he requested. I noticed him in the reflection of the large bathroom mirror. He smiled and watched intently. Just as I retracted the cord and put the hairdryer back on the hook, Charlie stood in the doorway. I turned around and smiled at him. He reached his hands out, inviting me to hug him and I did. His warmth was tempered by the pleasant hardness of his muscular body and growing manhood in his boxer shorts. He smelled my hair and ran his fingers through the warm, softness. He gently tugged on the back of my hair and kissed my neck. When he finally kissed my mouth, I thought I'd devour him. He gently moaned as I slipped my hands into the back of his boxer shorts and pulled him to me. I was about to move my hands to the front of his pants when he stopped me, taking each of my hands in his and putting them around his waist.

He slowly pulled his mouth from mine then reached up and touched my face with his right thumb and index finger. In almost a whisper he said, "You know, you shouldn't wear makeup, you don't need it." He was pushing my bangs from my eyes as he spoke.

"You're too kind," I smiled and went back to kissing him until he broke our kiss again.

"A nice way of saying you think I'm lying, huh?"

"Women like me *need* makeup," I said knowing full-well I didn't wear much makeup anyway.

"Women like you only *think* you need makeup," the sincerity in his tone made my heart melt just a little more.

"You are quite the charmer," I could feel myself blushing from the compliment.

"It's easy with you," he looked deep in my eyes as he spoke and pulled me to him. He kissed me slow and deep for several minutes before breaking our kiss again, "You're so comfortable with yourself and that is so sexy to me. I don't know if I've ever met anyone like you, Bianca." He sighed, "Now, come on." He took my hand in his and led me to the sofa.

"Look, there's a Star Trek marathon on right now." He sat down in the corner and invited me to sit in between his legs. I was a little surprised by the gesture but joined him. He wrapped his arms around me, "Is this OK?" I wasn't sure if he was referring to the television show or if I was comfortable but both were perfectly fine for me.

"Absolutely."

He kissed the back of my head and cuddled with me as we watched television. I'd never watched Star Trek, I just never had any desire. But honestly, I would have watched just about anything as long as I was watching it while in his arms. I wanted to ask, "When are we going to get to the sex?" Instead, I leaned back and just enjoyed his embrace.

Several "fan favorite" episodes later, I realized it was after eight o'clock and I was getting hungry. "Are you hungry?" I walked straight to the kitchen after having gotten up to go to the bathroom.

"I could eat," he said getting up, running his hands through his now dry hair. "Whatcha got?"

I quickly ran down the contents of my pantry in my mind as I stared blankly into the fridge. I closed the refrigerated side and swung open the freezer side.

"I hate to say it but I don't really have much. I usually shop on Sundays." I giggled and almost immediately had what I thought was a good idea.

"I have stuff for quesadillas." I snapped my fingers and re-opened the refrigerator door and pulled opened the drawer where I kept a zip top bag of Chihuahua cheese that I shredded myself a few days earlier. I pulled the bag out and saw there was plenty to make dinner. "And I could sauté some asparagus to go with it."

Charlie stood at the end of the counter and didn't say a word but I could see by the look on his face he wasn't interested in the offer.

"Or we can order a pizza." I put the cheese back and closed the door, "There's a really good New Jersey style place that delivers."

Charlie stayed silent as I leaned against the counter and waited for a reply, worrying that I'd suddenly done something wrong. It was like he was embarrassed to be with me.

"Uh – no," he said looking at the floor. "I should probably get going anyway," he picked up his clothes and headed for the bathroom.

Within a few minutes he dressed and rushed a "good bye", barely kissing me on the cheek.

"I'll call you." It was the last thing he said as the heavy, dark door of my apartment closed.

"OK," I said knowing he left in such a hurry he probably hadn't even heard my reply.

I never considered myself to be loose, I wasn't one to jump into bed with just anyone but I was truly surprised the night hadn't ended in sex. And sure, I'd only just met Charlie but we did spend the entire day together. It was probably the emotional equivalent of a few dates. What was most disturbing though was how suddenly he left. He'd gotten dressed so quickly that he hadn't even tucked in his shirt.

"Dammit," I said aloud to no one as I lie in bed and thought about it. "I shouldn't have ruined the mood. We were fine." I slapped the empty bedside and eventually fell asleep, the smell of him still lingering as an excruciating reminder of what I was missing.

When my alarm clock went off in the morning, I looked around searching for any sign that my Sunday hadn't been a dream. It wasn't until I got out of the shower that I got my evidence. Charlie had written on the mirror in the steam from the shower he had taken the night before. The steam from my shower revealed his message to me.

SMILE, BEAUTIFUL!

And I did.

It was already Thursday, four days later and I hadn't heard from him. I picked up the phone several times wanting to call him but placing the phone back on the receiver of my office phone before I'd dialed all nine numbers. I figured he was busy and Lynn agreed.

"Maybe you'll see him tonight?" Lynn smiled and watched me pick at my food as she finished her half of the hot braised chicken we'd ordered in for lunch.

I smiled and tried to act like it wasn't bothering me but it was all over my face. I wanted to hear from him, I wanted to see him and I couldn't wait for the day to be over. Maybe she was right? She had to be right. I'd see Charlie at the Westin. Of course.

And like any other Thursday, Lynn and I met up at the bar right after work. Ty and some of the others were already there in our usual booth so I ordered a drink then joined them. The minutes ticked by slowly and I found myself obsessing over the time. At five minutes after six o'clock, I was panicked. Elizabeth asked why I was so preoccupied, "You keep looking at your watch."

I politely avoided her question and continued to watch the door. Ten minutes later, Greg walked in without Charlie.

He ordered a drink and joined us, touching my shoulder and giving me a wink as he sat down next to me. I wanted to ask him where Charlie was but didn't want to give anything away.

"Charlie comes here once in a blue moon," I remembered Greg saying as he introduced us not quite a week earlier.

Everyone chatted on about their weekend plans while I sat silently, still watching the door.

"What's wrong?" Schicker asked putting his hand on my back as he spoke.

"Nothing," I feigned a smile and took another sip of the drink I'd been nursing for over an hour.

I was relieved when Charlie finally walked in half-hour later. I downed the last of my now mostly watered down vodka tonic and walked to the bar to get a new drink so I could greet him there. He barely looked at me, only casting a glance at me as I stood next to him waiting for our drinks. Charlie pointed to his glass and said "tab" to the bartender then quickly walked away and headed down the stairs.

Something was wrong.

I picked up my drink, walked down the stairs and across the dance floor to where Charlie stood looking for a proper pool cue.

"Hi," I said as I approached. I hadn't even gotten to the platform at the end of the dance floor where the pool tables and dart boards were when he answered with a terse, "Do you mind?"

He was rolling a pool stick on the table to check if it was straight.

"No, I don't mind," I didn't even take the step up onto the platform. "I'll just be at the table with everyone else," I stood waiting for him to look at me but he didn't. I shook my head and left him.

It was almost eight o'clock when Ty and Charlie returned from downstairs. Charlie said goodbye to the table as a group and left, never even looking in my direction. Lynn furrowed her brow and looked at me puzzled. I just sat there bewildered. "What the hell is going on?"

I thought to myself. I wanted to run out after him but didn't. Lynn shrugged her shoulders and suggested we go to the ladies' room.

As we exited the side door, Lynn asked, "What was that?"

"I have no idea," I turned to face her. "What could have happened between Sunday night and now?"

"And you haven't talked to him?"

"No. I would've told you," I felt myself starting to get upset.

"That's just weird," she said shaking her head. "Maybe he's just in a bad mood?" Lynn tried to sound hopeful.

"A bad mood is when someone snaps at you. Someone who ignores you is pissed."

I left shortly after Charlie left. It was getting late anyway and although I'd only seen him once, it somehow wasn't worth being there if he wasn't there.

I didn't sleep that night. I watched television, I tried to read, anything to help me pass the time. But after what seemed like days, it was barely after midnight.

"I'll just call him."

I rationalized it would be better to leave him a message at the office rather than try to call so late and possibly anger him more. I went to my laptop and opened my contacts list where he'd stored all of his information for me.

"Charlie, it's Bianca. It's Thursday night, well, just after midnight. I'm not sure what's going on but if you could please call me, I'd love to know what's wrong. I mean, I understand if you just don't want everyone to know our business but I was really surprised that...." I hesitated, *"I mean, you wouldn't even look at me. OK – well, I'm not gonna worry about this too much but I seriously can't imagine what I could have done to piss you off. But if I did, please just tell me what I did so I can make it up to you. OK? Call me."*

My awkward, rambling message was embarrassing and non-effective.

It was Friday evening and my usual excitement at going to the Westin was overshadowed by the dread of enduring another evening of being snubbed by Charlie Diaz. My insecurity was completely justified as he took advantage of every opportunity to look right through me.

It was after seven o'clock and almost two hours of being ignored by him proved to be too painful. I couldn't sit there hoping he'd suddenly change his demeanor and dismissed myself from our normal after work crowd. "Have a good weekend, everyone," I wasn't sure if anyone even heard me. It didn't matter.

Once again, during the wee small hours of the morning, I called and left a message on his office voice mail.

"Charlie, it's Bianca again. What happened? Why are you doing this? I just wanna know why you're so upset with me. I just wanna know what I did wrong. I don't know how to make it up to you if you won't let me. Please call me. Please tell me what I did."

I tried hard not to let the overwhelming rejection resonate in every syllable but it almost certainly did.

Lynn called me Saturday afternoon but I still didn't have an answer for her.

"He hasn't called or sent an email or anything?" I could hear one of her sons and Ty talking in the background.

"No. And I don't know what else to do." My head pounded from too much sleep and the Tylenol PM I'd taken hung with me even until this late hour of the afternoon.

"Want me to ask Ty if he knows anything?" Lynn asked tentatively.

"Would you?" I was suddenly hopeful.

"OK – I'll ask if he knows anything."

"I hate to get you involved but I'm just – I don't know what else to do."

"Well, you didn't ask me, I offered and if it feels weird, I'll back off," her tone was suddenly almost a whisper and I could tell she was trying to make sure Ty didn't hear the conversation. "But it's not like he doesn't know something's up. Everyone knows –" she stopped herself.

"Everyone knows what?"

"Well, everyone knows something's wrong. Even Brandi, the bartender, asked what was going on when you left last night."

"Great," I rolled my eyes, "just great."

"Don't worry. I'll talk to Ty and we'll see. OK? Right now, I gotta go."

I returned to bed. The only way time was going to pass was if I was asleep. Lynn didn't call the rest of the weekend. Did she talk to Ty? Was it that bad? And if it was, did I really want to know?

* * *

Monday morning came and I wasn't in such a hurry to get to the office. Somehow I knew I wasn't going to like what she had to say. When I got there and saw the look on her face, I could see she wasn't excited to tell me. And maybe I didn't want to know but I *had* to know.

Lynn and I avoided each other as long as possible but lunch time came and there weren't any distractions. The guys left the office as they usually did, leaving us there alone with too much privacy to avoid the conversation we'd apparently both been dreading.

I pushed my fork around the salad I'd brought for lunch. Lynn raised her fork slowly, taking only small bites of snap peas that came with her lunch.

I finally broke the silence, "OK – give it to me, Lynn."

It wasn't that anything she told me was a lie. It just seemed like she was talking about something that happened to someone else. The tone she used made me think she was being gentle in her retelling of a story she'd already heard from me but without any of chemistry I'd described to her with the giddiness of a teenaged girl. That Monday morning after my day with Charlie, I giggled and glowed about how much we liked each other and what a connection we had and my confidence in the connection between us convinced her it must have been true.

"That's pretty much it." She carefully wiped the corners of her mouth so as not to smudge the flawless makeup on her cocoa dark skin, averting her eyes as she folded the thin, white napkin and tucking it neatly under the Styrofoam container that held her lunch.

I inhaled and tried to understand what she was trying to say without saying it. Charlie told Ty we'd spent the day looking at apartments, had something to eat then hung out at my apartment for a while. All true. But in the version I told Lynn on Monday morning, I didn't leave out the details. I told her of the attraction between us. I didn't skip over the part where he accosted me the moment he arrived at my apartment. I didn't forget to tell her how he felt me up in the bathroom of the model unit or how he showered at my place and cuddled with me wearing only his boxers. I didn't fail to mention the note he left on the mirror.

I could see by the look on her face and the fact that she was avoiding eye contact, she had more to say and just didn't know how. Or didn't want to. My mind jumped around – one second I was thinking, "So, he doesn't kiss and tell. This is a good thing." The next minute I was reminding myself that he left suddenly and hadn't contacted me since.

Thus, the reason I'm sitting in awkward silence with my friend while we both pick at a lunch that normally we'd devour while lively chatting about our favorite soap opera or the season's newest trends in fashion. I knew my friend well enough to know there was more that was making her uncomfortable and I should probably let it go but something in me made me blurt out the question in spite of my good judgment.

"Was that it?"

She drummed two fingers on the table and took a moment to collect her thoughts. That's when I knew it was going to be worse than I expected. She only drummed the ring and middle finger on her right hand when she was really uneasy with the news she was about to deliver. I'd seen it when she told me she was going to have to take a leave of absence because they'd found a lump in her breast. I'd seen it when she told me she was being promoted and would be my new boss. This was obviously something she felt was going to upset me.

38

"Bianca, let me just say something. I love you and care about you as my friend and I respect you as my colleague," she drew in a deep breath, "so anything that has to do with anyone else won't ever interfere with us, OK?"

"Of course not," I tried to sound positive but with the serious tone of her voice I couldn't be sure if it was actually true. "I don't want anything to ever come between us." I turned up the corners of my mouth and tried to smile even though she wasn't looking at me.

"Bianca, you've been an amazing friend to me. You were new here and I kinda threw you to the wolves with my illness but you handled things with a grace and professionalism beyond your years. And you've been a wonderful friend to me, bringing me casseroles and fresh-baked cookies when I was going through my treatments. Being so considerate of my family," she sighed, "my boys never ate so good as when you were plying them with your tuna noodle casserole and baked ziti. If it wasn't for you, they would've lived off of sandwiches and Spaghetti-O's. I couldn't even think about making food, much less have the energy." She smiled and finally looked up at me, "No one else thinks about people like you do. And I've never known anyone as genuinely thoughtful in the things they do for others. I mean that."

"My friends are important to me."

She nodded.

"Lynn, you can tell me. I can handle it. I promise."

I could see her almost hold her breath, "Charlie said you're not really his type."

"That's it?" Now, I was holding my breath.

She exhaled slowly, "He told Ty you were kinda slutty and not really his type."

I was momentarily stunned to silence.

"He called me a slut?" I felt myself get light-headed. I tried several times to form some intelligible sentence to express my disbelief to no avail. The words just wouldn't come.

Lynn continued, "I believe everything you told me, OK? But Charlie's version's different."

I replayed different moments of the day in my mind and wondered if he was right. Had I done something too slutty? Is that why he left so suddenly?

"I know what you're doing, girl. Don't do it. Just forget it. He's an asshole."

"Is he?" I asked with warm tears of embarrassment starting to sting my eyes, "Do you know Charlie to be anything other than a gentleman?"

"If he led you on then blew you off, he's the asshole here, leave it at that," she got up and put the leftover of her food in the refrigerator and returned to the table. She wiped the area immediately in front of her with a fresh napkin, "No need to think about it too much. Just forget about him."

"So, you got the impression he's never gonna speak to me again? That's it? He gets to grope me for an entire day and then walk away?"

"I just think you should let it go," she said averting her eyes from mine again. "It's not worth it."

"What else did he say, Lynn?"

She sighed, "He wants you to stop bothering him. Or something like that."

"Are you fucking kidding me?" I stopped myself and got up from the kitchen table. I scrunched the Styrofoam container closed and angrily shoved it in the garbage on my way out of the kitchen. Without another word, I headed through the doorway to my desk.

"Bianca," Lynn called out after me, "I'm sorry but I thought you should know."

I couldn't face her. There was no facing anyone at this moment. After reaching my desk, I stood there, looking at the clock on my phone and seeing lunchtime wasn't quite over. "I need some air," I headed for the front door of our office suite.

Lynn followed out after me as I strode to the stairwell, "Are you coming back?"

"Just give me 10 minutes."

"Sure," her voice was faint, "take your time."

I trotted down the stairs and angrily hit the slap bar that unlocked the door, swinging it wide open in the process. I walked out the front of our building, the first floor being a bustling bank and wondered what I'd do, when I recognized a familiar face. We usually only saw each other in the parking lot and nodded politely to each other but at this moment he had something I needed.

"Hey, I've never introduced myself. I'm Bianca, I work at –" He interrupted and explained he knew who I was.

"I'm Josh," he held a cigarette in his teeth and held out his hand to shake mine.

"Nice to meet you," I smiled at him and shook his hand although I was seething inside. "Can I bum a smoke?"

"Yeah, sure," he pulled a pack from his front shirt pocket and handed it to me. "You need a light?"

I nodded and he obliged. The first inhale hit my lungs like acid and I tried hard to keep myself from coughing. It had been months since I'd had a cigarette but I'd never wanted one as badly as I did in the moment I saw Josh standing there ashing his. After the third or fourth drag, it was like I'd never stopped smoking and I felt the calm, light-headed feeling I needed so desperately. I tilted my head back and enjoyed it.

"Wow, you're really enjoying that cigarette." The boyish grin on his face made me think I might be enjoying it a little too much.

I composed myself and looked at the burning white stick I held in my left hand and took another drag, "Let's just say, I've had a rough week."

"And it's only Monday," he said crushing the butt of his cigarette into the black sand of the tall ash tray that stood waist-high in the corner. "I gotta get back in there, you want another?" He showed me the mostly-full pack.

"No. Thank you though," I begged off, "this is perfect for now." I took another drag.

"OK. Well, it was good meeting you finally," he shook my hand again. "See ya 'round," he flashed a smile and pushed his way through the revolving door.

Even though his back was turned to me, I waved and took another drag of my cigarette.

The rest of the afternoon passed slowly and I asked Lynn if I could leave a half-hour early. She had a look of guilt on her face when she granted my request.

"See you tomorrow," I said as the door clicked close behind me.

On my way home, I picked up a 12-pack of beer and pack of my brand of menthol cigarettes at a local mini-mart. I hadn't had either in my apartment since moving to D.C. I then rushed home and began seeking oblivion. The words of a Madonna song echoed in my head as I sat alone on the sofa and drank.

"Indeed, it's not even six o'clock and I'm drunk," I lit a cigarette and chugged the rest of the beer I had in front of me.

* * *

The next several weeks passed painfully slow. Tommy repeatedly questioned if I was alright and commented on me being "too quiet".

"I just have a lot on my mind," was my standard answer.

One morning, he had an appointment at the Department of Energy and didn't make it back in time to join the other half-dozen engineers in the office for lunch as was his usual. He walked in with a foot long sandwich in a brown bag from a deli down the street, "Wanna split this with me? I can't get through this whole thing."

I told him I already had something for lunch but joined him in the kitchen so we could eat together. Anymore, I ate lunch alone since Lynn and Ty usually met for lunch somewhere. I thought it might be nice to have some company. Tom worked through the sandwich as I picked at my microwave meal.

Swallowing a large bite, he wiped his mouth, "So, you haven't moved out of the apartment yet?"

I took my time chewing so I could try to formulate a reasonable answer. I didn't have one. I hadn't moved out of my apartment and had abandoned my search for an apartment since the one day I went looking with Charlie.

He took another bite and spoke with his mouth half-full, "And you're working round-the-clock on projects that aren't even due yet," he chewed his food quickly and looked at me still waiting for me to say something.

I stabbed more food with my fork and stayed silent.

"C'mon, what's going on?"

I did the best I could to explain without really explaining anything that I was going through some changes and just needed time to think.

He smiled, "When you wanna talk, I'll be here for you."

I wanted to hug him. I wanted to cry into his chest. I wanted to tell him how the rejection from Charlie Diaz, whom I only knew for one day, had devastated my self-esteem but I knew I couldn't. He didn't need to know this. He didn't want to know this. For that matter, neither did I.

And just as I started to thank him for his friendship and always being so kind to me, our colleagues walked in from lunch and immediately began a conversation about his meeting at DOE, giving me the perfect chance to slip away without another word.

I started going to the bar four or five days a week. I told myself it was because of traffic or boredom but the truth was I wanted to see Charlie. I hoped if I made myself more available he would finally break his silence and talk to me.

I was wrong.

And even though I was told when I first met him he was only there "once in a blue moon", Charlie was suddenly at the bar as often as I was. Unfortunately, the tension between us was driving a wedge into the group of friends we shared. It was as if they had to choose between us and it quickly appeared the group preferred Charlie. I wasn't sure if it was because he'd known them longer, was more in their age group or maybe he was simply more likeable than me but when Charlie was there, no one – and that included Greg Schicker – had much to say to me. Everyone was polite enough but as soon as Charlie arrived, the guys would take off and shoot pool or play darts, leaving me sitting alone.

Lynn saw Ty every day at lunch and had two kids at home, the other ladies in our group had families and didn't usually hang out except on Friday's, so I would sit there perched atop a barstool, nursing a drink, while watching the guys play their game of choice. I tried not to watch Charlie exclusively but I couldn't help it. And when I noticed his beer running low, I'd wait for him to come buy another round and hope he'd talk to me. He never did. The most I got was a nod of acknowledgement once when I made eye contact with him as he climbed the stairs.

It had been almost three months since my one and only day with Charlie and I was spending more and more time at the bar and when not there, drinking at home alone. I had completely abandoned my search for an apartment, choosing not to think what it would take to furnish and support a new home. Instead, the almost two thousand dollars a month for rent seemed reasonable by comparison.

* * *

It was just before four o'clock on Thursday afternoon when my office phone rang. My heart almost stopped when I recognized the exchange. It was Greg Schicker.

"So you were expecting someone else, huh?" He said as I answered the phone.

"What's up? How are you?" I tried to hide the disappointment in my voice.

We chatted for a few minutes. He mentioned he'd just gotten back from seeing his family in Atlanta and that he was swamped at work.

"Wanna catch a movie tomorrow night?"

It wasn't a movie I had any interest in and none of the actors were very well-known but I agreed. I thought it was odd that he chose such a late show time and a theater so far away but I had nothing else to do.

The movie was surprisingly enjoyable and I thanked him for suggesting it. "I'm glad you liked it," he flashed a smile then looked at his watch. "You wanna go get some cheesecake?"

I knew it had to be close to midnight. I looked at my watch, "It might be a little late for cheesecake."

"Oh, live a little," he said opening the car door for me. He got in the driver's seat and turned over the ignition, waiting for my answer, "Cheesecake? Yes or no?"

"If you can find me coffee, I might be willing to have a piece of cheesecake with it," I smiled my first genuine smile in weeks.

We drove a short distance from the theater to a nearby mall. As we got past the vestibule, I saw a familiar face.

"Hey, Bianca. How are you?" It was Adam, Lynn's oldest son. He was wearing his uniform and appeared to have just gotten out of work. He gave me a hug and I introduced him to Greg. Greg, suddenly nervous, tried to rush us off but it was too late.

"You're not going to the party?"

I looked over at Greg just as he looked away, "We just came from the movies."

He nodded, "Well, I just talked to Mom, she and Ty just got there." He chuckled, "Get this, she wanted to make sure I was gonna be home in time to make sure Marcus got home for curfew."

I faked a laugh with him, "You couldn't get him home before curfew unless you bribed him with cash."

We laughed for a moment while Greg stood there nervously shifting in his shoes.

"Well, have fun." He gave me another quick hug, "Nice to meet you, Sir." Adam held his hand up in a wave and began walking away, "Talk to you later."

"So that's what this was about? Making sure I don't go to the party."

"No, I wanted to go out. We only ever see each other at the bar and –"

"You're a lousy fucking liar," my voice echoed in the nearly empty mall. I turned and started to walk out. Greg followed me to the parking lot.

"Where's the party?" I asked, not even turning to face him.

"Montgomery Village," he said solemnly as he caught up and walked next to me.

I let out a sarcastic laugh, "At Elizabeth's house? That's fantastic." I waited for him to unlock the door with the remote as we reached the car, "I guess Charlie plans on being there?" I had my back to him with my hand on the handle waiting to hear the telltale sound of the door being unlocked.

"We're here now, let's get some cheesecake. We can talk."

"Please, just take me home," the tone in my voice was one of a demand more than a request.

Greg and I rode back to my apartment in silence. As soon as we pulled into the parking lot he began to explain or maybe apologize but I told him I didn't need to hear it. As he pulled to the front of my building he asked if I was going to be OK but I got out of the car before he finished the question.

I didn't know it at the time but I'd see Greg again later that night. We'd run into each other a couple hours later at a townhouse in Montgomery Village.

I took a long, hot shower and considered whether or not I should call Lynn. I wondered why she hadn't mentioned the party. It was only after obsessing over it for an hour that I decided to call. She told me she thought I knew about the party and had simply chosen my date with Greg.

"I'm not even sure I'm invited," I said brushing my now almost dry hair away from my face. "Are you sure it's cool?"

"Get your ass over here," she said with a slight slur and I could tell even though she was tipsy, she was sincere. She gave me directions and said she'd expect me soon.

I decided to glam it up a little bit. I wore tall, strappy heels, a low-cut shirt and a full-face of makeup. I took a look at my reflection in the mirror, realizing my friends hadn't seen me in anything other than my regular work attire. Was I trying too hard? Did I look slutty? I chased the thoughts from my head, "Fuck you, Charlie Diaz." I shoved my driver's license in the back pocket of my jeans, grabbed my keys and headed for the Village.

As I arrived to Elizabeth's house I started to worry. I technically wasn't invited but when I walked in, she hugged me and said she was glad to see me. She apologized for not extending the formal invitation and said she didn't want any trouble.

I felt guilty that she even felt the need to say that.

"Come in, get a drink, have fun," she said smiling and kissing me on the cheek.

I wandered around the house, occasionally running into a familiar face and striking up a conversation for a few minutes before moving on in search of Lynn. When Lynn saw me descending the basement stairs she jumped up from the card table where she sat with three other people and trotted to me immediately hugging my neck, "I'm so sorry, girl. I should have asked you if you were coming, I shouldn't have assumed anything. I know all this shit's been rough on you."

She was hugging me so tightly, I had to gently push her away, "It's fine." I rubbed her arms, "So, you winning?"

"Hell, no," she laughed.

Ty walked over and put his arm around my shoulder, "You look good, kid." He gave me a quick kiss on the cheek.

"Yeah, you do," Lynn wailed, "I was just thinking that. You look sexy." The way she dragged out the last syllable of the word "sexy" told me she had indeed had quite a bit to drink. I didn't worry because I knew Ty would take good care of her. I was happy to see her enjoying herself.

I laughed off the compliment and settled into a convenient out-of-the-way place to watch the game. In between hands, Lynn started to get up to get another drink. "I'm empty," she said finishing the last bit of the beer in the bottle she held in her hand.

I wasn't playing and hadn't gotten anything to drink for myself since I'd arrived, so I offered to get her another drink, "Let me get it."

Ty waved at me and winked, "Can you grab me a shot, hun? Anything's fine."

I nodded and proceeded up the stairs to the bar, taking Lynn's empty with me. The self-appointed bartender poured me a shot of top shelf tequila and told me the beers were in the fridge.

I walked in the kitchen and rinsed the empty beer bottle and deposited it in the blue container marked "recycle only" that stood in the far corner of the kitchen. Just as I turned around, the door from the back deck opened and there stood Greg. I waited for him to say something but he didn't. He just stepped out of the way and as he did, I caught a glimpse of Charlie behind him. I walked over to the fridge but didn't say anything. I got my friend her beer and headed down to the basement. I tried to be strong, at least until I was out of sight of Charlie but I could feel myself trembling. I must have looked upset because as Ty stood up and took the mostly full shot glass from my hand he looked around the basement, "Charlie here?"

I nodded and handed Lynn her beer, "I gotta go." I turned to leave and in my haste almost knocked someone over. I collected my wits then walked the stairs as quickly as I could in the shoes I was wearing.

Greg met me at the top step, "Can we talk?"

"Not now," I walked past him to the kitchen. To my own amazement, instead of leaving out the door Greg and Charlie had just come in, I reached into the fridge and grabbed a beer. I stood looking out the kitchen window into the darkness wondering if I could really be in the same house with Charlie and not ask for an explanation. After weeks of phone calls and emails asking, practically begging him to tell me what I'd done wrong, I'd finally given up. But I also knew myself. And I knew I still wanted that explanation. I still had that neurotic need to know.

I was about half done with my beer when over the loud music I thought I heard Greg talking to someone. I heard a voice raised in what sounded like anger and turned around to find Greg standing with his back to me, his right hand holding the frame of doorway, Charlie standing directly in front of him. Charlie adjusted his glasses, saying nothing, only staring at me. He took a few steps backward, glancing first at

Greg, then me, before turning around and disappearing into the large crowd of people in the living room. I threw a look at Greg then turned back around and continued drinking my beer, staring out the window in silence.

I considered leaving, realizing I wasn't really socializing with anyone and now really uncomfortable because Charlie was there. I suppose it was the stubborn part of me that decided to stay. After all, Elizabeth said she was happy to see me and my best friend was there. *"Why should I leave?"*

I rinsed my now empty bottle, put it in the recycling and grabbed another before leaving the kitchen. I had every intention of joining Lynn and Ty in the basement but had to go to the bathroom. I asked someone where the bathrooms were and was told the only functioning one was on the 2nd floor.

At the top of the stairs, there was a bedroom down a long hall to my left. It was there I spotted Charlie through the open door, sitting on a daybed picking the label off of his bottled beer. To my right were two other bedrooms and the people in line waiting for the bathroom that was almost directly in front of me. Without hesitation, I walked to the room where Charlie sat, closing the door behind me. As though he was expecting me, Charlie stayed quiet, not even looking up as I entered the room.

In a discreet voice, I began my plea, "I know this isn't the right time or place but I just have to ask you, what did I do – "

"Bianca, you need to get over it," he was still picking at the shiny label and dropping tiny ripped pieces of paper into the empty bottle. He spoke in a matter-of-fact tone and didn't look at me.

"I just don't understand what I did. I mean, everything was fine and then all of a sudden you leave and I never hear from you again?" I still spoke in a quiet voice and stood my ground near the door. "What did I do that was so wrong? I mean, I just wanna know because I honestly have no idea how we could have such a great time together and then you never speak to me again. Don't I deserve to know the truth?"

That's when he got angry, "Just fucking leave me alone!" He stood up and got close to me as I stood partially blocking the door, "There's *nothing* between us." His emphasis on the word "nothing" was especially cruel.

"OK," I swallowed hard, "but can't you just tell me why you're so mad at me?" We were so close I could smell his aftershave. I was tempted to touch him, longing to have his arms around me again, remind him how good it felt when we were together that one perfect day. "I know you like me, Charlie. I know it. I feel it. At the bar, I feel you trying to ignore me. I feel you trying to ignore the chemistry between us. You can't. And neither can I." I leaned slightly closer to him, "You can say there's nothing between us but that's a lie and you know it." I could feel every muscle in my body tighten as I spoke so boldly the words I barely allowed myself to think.

He stared fire into my eyes then practically shouted in my face, "Stop emailing me. Stop calling me. Just leave me the fuck alone."

Despite my best effort to suppress them, tears began to stream down my face. He stepped around me and I instinctively got out of the way as he swung the door open, "By the way, you look like a slut with all that makeup." A last parting shot.

I rushed to the mirror above the dresser, out of sight of the open door and tried for several minutes to wipe the dark streaks of mascara off of my cheeks as the tears continued through the heavy makeup on my face. Realizing it was a losing battle, I quickly raced down the stairs and out the back door. I took the stairs from the deck down to the back yard as quickly as I could in the shoes I was wearing, cursing myself for wearing them as the heels dug into the soft lawn under my feet. I trotted up the side of the house and crossed the front yard toward my car. Charlie was on the front stoop with Schicker and a few others, lighting up a cigar, I thought I heard someone say my name but I didn't stop.

* * *

Early Monday morning, Lynn transferred a call to me, it was Elizabeth. She explained that her cousin, Viv, had been in line for the bathroom during my confrontation with Charlie. She apologized for the scene as best she could before I interrupted her.

"Elizabeth, it's not your fault. I'm just sorry that my friends are more uncomfortable about this than he is," I slowly exhaled and tried to hide my own embarrassment.

"Well, he's an asshole and that was totally uncalled for. As far as I'm concerned, he disrespected one of my guests – "

I interrupted again, "I provoked him. I shouldn't have confronted him. It wasn't the time or the place. I'm so sorry."

This time Elizabeth interrupted me, "Look, I know you guys have had your differences and there are various stories floating around out there but I don't care. It wasn't right and I just wanted to apologize."

We talked for another several minutes and agreed to have a drink on Friday. I didn't have the heart to tell her that I wasn't even sure I'd go back to the Westin. She didn't have to know if I ever intended to take her up on her offer, she just had to know that I accepted it. After what happened, I figured it wasn't such a good idea for me to knowingly be anywhere Charlie Diaz would be. The way he looked at me when he told me I looked like a slut, that was the look of someone who had genuine disdain for me. It was like he flipped a switch and was suddenly furious with me. I grew up with that kind of volatility. I knew it well and I knew it could be dangerous.

On Thursday afternoon, Lynn asked if I would be going "up the road", our code for the bar inside the Westin. I told her I wasn't sure if it was a good idea.

"Well, don't do anything that's gonna make you uncomfortable," Lynn said turning off her desk light and heading for the door. "But remember this, Charlie's the one that showed his ass, there's no reason you should feel bad."

I couldn't accept that. To me, what happened at the party was entirely my fault and could have been avoided. Greg had taken me out to distract me, to keep me away, knowing Charlie would be there and knowing I would confront him with the question that had almost become an obsession.

"Why?"

The more I thought about it, the more I realized, I'd mishandled everything that night. Not only with Charlie but with Greg.

Greg didn't deserve how I'd treated him, he was being a friend. And I absolutely deserved the backlash I got for my persistence. It was wrong of me all around and I felt like I owed everyone an apology about everything.

I thought on it and decided not to join Lynn that night or the next. In fact, I decided right then to take a little bit of time to focus on something other than the fact that I felt like shit over what Charlie Diaz thought of me. Hanging out in a bar full of his friends wasn't the place for me to be right now. Maybe I could let some time pass, stop feeling the rejection like knife in the gut every time I thought about him. It was clear to me, after what happened at Elizabeth's house, I was the one with the problem.

I knew there were other areas of my life that I'd been neglecting. Or maybe it's called wallowing? Either way, it was time I actually started thinking about something other than Charlie Diaz.

* * *

It had been over two weeks since the party at Elizabeth's house. I started focusing on finding a new place to live and spent most of my free time looking for a suitable, affordable place. It helped too that work was busy and I was exhausted after working back-to-back 70-hour weeks.

We'd just met another Friday night deadline and sent the drill off with the team when Lynn suggested we go out for a drink. And where else but "up the road"? She called Ty to see if he wanted to meet us but he said he'd started feeling the effects of the flu. I called Greg but got voicemail, so I left a message letting him know we'd probably be at the Westin sometime around ten o'clock.

It was strangely familiar, Lynn and I walking into the bar, deafening music thumping, crowds of people we didn't usually see since we were usually only there during "happy hour". I smiled, "I'm glad we decided to come." I shoved her playfully with one shoulder as we stood at the very crowded bar waiting for our order.

After our first drink, I left Lynn at the bar with our purses while I went to the ladies' room. I walked out the side door and down the steps to the bathrooms that were a short walk down the hall. The lobby echoed with the busy sounds of hotel guests checking in and milling about. I smiled to myself thinking how nice it was to not feel a pit in my stomach being there.

As I left the stall and walked forward to the sinks, I noticed two women standing just to the side of the entry of the bathroom. The women spoke to each other as I washed my hands, the running water keeping me from hearing anything they were saying even if I was trying to listen. I smiled and said, "hi" to the strangers as I started past them to the door.

"You're Bianca, right?" The taller of the two blondes asked. She looked like a cross between an aerobics instructor and a District Attorney. She was somewhere in her late 30's and had a very muscular body that her exceptionally-tailored black suit accentuated nicely. The shorter of the two women was probably a little younger, fit but not to the same level as her friend. She was wearing a black pencil skirt and tight pink top that exposed cleavage that I could only describe as "Barbie Doll boobs", not nearly as well done or natural-looking as the breast augmentations I'd seen when I lived in Los Angeles.

My heart began pounding in my chest and I felt my fists instinctively clench, "Do I know you?"

"Stop bothering Charlie Diaz," the shorter woman snapped.

"Excuse me," I said trying to walk by two women, "I have to go."

"What you have to do," the woman in the suit said, "is leave Charlie alone." She turned me around by my hand closest to her.

"Don't touch me," I jerked my hand from hers.

"He's not trying to fuck a skank like you, OK?" She and her friend shoved their way by me.

"What the fuck?" I said out of instinct as the women left. I gave myself a moment to process what had just happened before leaving the bathroom. Having not seen or even attempted to contact Charlie in weeks, I was shocked beyond words. My thoughts raced, how would these women know me? How would they know I was even at the bar? Especially this late and for the fact that it was only Lynn and I that were there.

Then it dawned on me, Charlie must be in the bar.

Somewhere.

I rushed back and told Lynn what happened. I felt my eyes were big as saucers as I described the women, "Well, the one was really fit in a really nice black Gucci suit. Or at least, I think it's Gucci. Either way, it looked really expensive." I took a sip of my second drink the bartender had just put down in front of me, "The other one was a little shorter, bleach blonde also but wearing a pink shirt with a black skirt," I looked around the bar, searching for them, concerned about another ambush.

"This is bullshit," she said scanning the room with me.

"Lynn, you know, I told you, I haven't been around and I haven't even attempted to contact him since the card party. I swear – "

Lynn interrupted, "Is that Charlie down there?" She pointed to one of the tables on the perimeter of the dance floor.

The Gucci suit blonde stood next to him, the other woman stood on the opposite side of the table. Charlie met my eyes with his and grimaced as the blonde standing next to him began kissing him.

I turned my back on the trio, "I swear, I had no idea he was here."

"This is totally weird," she continued sipping her drink.

"When you talked to Greg earlier, he didn't say anything about Charlie being here?" She was trying to be pleasant in her doubts of me.

"I got his voicemail. I left a message, that's it," I tried not to sound as insulted as I was.

"Sorry," she acquiesced, "it's just strange. Not the part about Charlie being here but why would those bitches jump you like that?" She put down her half empty vodka-tonic.

"They didn't exactly jump me but they sure were making a point," I hadn't even told my friend exactly what was said in the short but humiliating confrontation. "Can we just hurry up and finish these? I wanna go." I could feel the temptation to confront Charlie and his posse welling up inside of me. I knew from what happened last time, it would not be a good idea and I didn't exactly want to end up in physical fight with anyone.

Lynn and I didn't speak again of the strange happenings that night but we also didn't discuss anything having to do with the Westin or anyone we knew from there, except her boyfriend, Ty. We still socialized outside of work, doing our usual brunch thing on Sundays when we could but it was as if we never went to the bar. I wasn't offended though. I knew Lynn and I were alright, that was all that was important to me. I knew if anything happened, she'd tell me.

For my part, I was busy settling into my new home.

I met Elle one Sunday afternoon as I was leaving a particularly desirable neighborhood on the fringe of Germantown. I'd stopped in a grocery store after a long morning of apartment scouting to buy a few bottles of water and a box of cereal bars. I'd thought about stopping at the convenient store on the opposite side of the street but figured it would be less expensive and make more sense to wander through the store and see what kind of people were there at that time of day. The petite redhead was attempting to hang a bright pink piece of paper among the cluttered postings in the foyer of the store.

"Shit!" She yelled in exasperation as she reached as high as she could on her tip-toes, then collapsed back to her feet.

"Just take some of that other crap down," I suggested as I paused and waited for her to move out of the direct path of the exit.

"You're right," she said contemplating what ads to remove.

"Yeah, if you put it too high, short people like you won't be able to read it."

We giggled together for a moment.

She then shrugged and sighed, "I know this is old-school but I'm desperate." She flashed the paper toward me so I could see in big block letters, **ROOM FOR RENT**. "I don't suppose you're looking for a place to live?" She smiled and introduced herself, "I'm Rachelle Kramer but please don't ever call me Rachelle, I hate that name. I go by Elle. Damn. I'm downright screwed, I know it. I don't know what else to do."

"I'm Bianca – "

She interrupted, "I love that name." She immediately sighed, "I don't suppose you're looking for a roommate? That's what all this is about." She handed me the paper which I quickly scanned. "My biggest issue is that I'm getting married in a year so whatever roommate I have has to understand. I mean, it would be a place for the next year or so, maybe a little more if you needed extra time. Listen to me, going on and on." She took a step back to let me pass, inadvertently blocking a woman walking in from the opposite direction. "Geez. I'm just in the way," the chatty woman was suddenly somber.

"Actually, Elle, I am looking for a place to live. I just hadn't considered the roommate thing. I haven't lived with anyone for a really long time."

"Well, our place – well, it's my place but really our place because my fiancé and I bought it even though our wedding is so far away because we got such a smokin' deal on it and didn't want to pass it up so we went ahead and bought it but he doesn't live there, although he does stay over sometimes. It's just right down the road and I'm only looking at $500 a month including everything because I know it's going to be a hassle for my roomie to have to move in another year but D.C. is kind of a transient area so I was thinking this short-term thing should work out for someone, not necessarily a transient but you know what I mean. And so far I've had zero luck. And as the wedding planning kicks into high gear, I'm gonna be spending a lot of time with my Mom doing wedding stuff so I kinda need someone I can trust Lucy with – Lucy's my cat. She's a sweetheart but I'd hate to board her, you know? Do you have any pets? This may seem a little forward of me but I would love it if you wanted to stop by, just as something to consider if you can't find your own place."

I stood there quiet for a split second but before I could answer, she continued, "I know I'm talking 100 miles an hour but my other really big issue is I'm leaving Tuesday for three weeks. And I've kinda been putting this off and told my fiancé I would get this thing under control so now, well, I'm a crazy person."

"Elle, I would love to come see the house and 12 months is not a problem for me. I could plan to be out before your new husband moves in."

"Oh my gosh, you're an angel! I'll give you directions," she flipped over the bright paper she'd just been attempting to hang and drew a crude map. The house wasn't far from the store, just a quick couple of lefts and rights.

"I'll meet you there," I waved to her as I reached my vehicle, coincidentally parked in the same row as hers. I drove down Great Seneca Highway feeling a strange connection to Elle. Something in the tone of her voice or the kindness in her eyes told me she was going to be my new roommate.

We soon arrived to the beautiful, white, ranch style house with a very long, winding driveway. There was an extra pad of blacktop to the right of the over-sized two-car garage that looked like it could accommodate another two, maybe even three cars and I decided to park there. I was just getting out of my car when Elle called out from the garage. "Over here," she closed the door of her bright red, late-model Audi coupe and fumbled with her keys, "Lucy goes crazy when the front door opens." She led the way through the door inside the garage.

The door led into a large eat-in kitchen that had a cozy, country vibe. To the right, I could see what looked like a formal dining table littered with stacks of magazines and legal pads. As we passed the kitchen table on the left, I could see the front door and then the huge living room. On the far wall was a large sliding glass door that led to a large deck accessible from both the living room and the master suite.

"Come on in," she hung her keys on a hook that was on a partial wall between the kitchen and living room, "I'll show you around."

The open floor plan was light and inviting. There were two bedrooms on the main level and a large bathroom, a bit further down the hall on the right was a master suite that had a full bathroom. "Obviously, this is my room," she flipped on the lights to show off the ceiling fan and lighting fixture that made an immediate impact on airflow in the room, the oversized blades turning slowly, creating a pleasant breeze. "One of these is a guest bedroom and the other is Dave's office," she led the way back down the hall to the stairs near the front door that wound slightly to the finished walk-out basement. The basement had a "man cave" feel featuring lots of dark wood, a stone hearth in front of a brick fireplace and a large sofa. "I had this bar custom-built for Dave as an engagement present slash housewarming present." She walked over to the impressive ebonized cherry structure and ran her hands proudly over the counter. "But here, let me show you the room. It's not much but you'd have a lot of privacy down here and you could use anything in the house you want. I work a lot and like I said, I will likely spend some long weekends out-of-town while I'm doing the major wedding planning stuff but not like you can't have a life because you need to cat sit or anything like that but if I did have someone I could trust that was here some of the time with Lucy that would be a load off my mind. My other option is to take her to my Mom's and then bring her back after we get married but I hate to do that. I've had her since I was in college and I would miss her too much. I don't know, I know it's probably a lot to ask if you're not an animal person." We walked to the far side of the basement, stopping briefly to see the large bathroom, "As you can see, you'd have your own full bathroom. It's got plenty of storage under the sink and that," she pointed at a closed door in the corner next to the shower, "is a linen closet. So there's lots of room for towels and extra toilet paper and whatnot." There was natural light coming through the frosted glass window high on the wall of the shower that had a hinged glass door and was fully tiled. "No bathtub though, I hope that's not a problem."

"Not at all."

We walked another couple of feet to a closed door, "I keep this closed so Lucy doesn't hang out in here," she opened the door, stepped in and then out of the way so I could enter. "This is the room. You can see it's furnished but if you have your own stuff, I could move all this out."

"Elle, I don't know what to say," I admired the expanse of the tastefully decorated room. There was a queen size bed to my right with a nightstand next to the wall with a lamp and petite Howard Miller clock. To the left was an entire wall of closets with sliding doors. I walked to a chest of drawers that stood next to beige chaise that sat on an angle in the corner, "This is lovely."

She flipped the light switches, engaging a ceiling fan and light fixture identical to the one in her bedroom, "Yeah it's nice. We like it. We originally thought Dave and I would move in together before we got married but after much debate, we decided not to. And since we're spending a significant amount of money on the wedding, it's like, why not? You know? But if I'm honest, it's more about just not feeling so lonely. It'll just be nice to know someone else is around. Not like you have to be around all the time, that's not what I mean. It just gets too quiet sometimes, you know?"

"I know exactly what you mean," I nodded and looked around the room. The only window in the room was at the identical height of the one in the shower and was on the wall near the bed, too high to see out of without some effort.

She must have noticed that it caught my eye, "I know. The only thing is there isn't a lot of light except for this time of day but it's not like you have to be confined to this room, you basically have the entire basement to yourself. And the bar has a mini-fridge and cabinets so you could store whatever you might want there and I can get you a microwave if you want one so you don't have to go upstairs every time you need something."

"Elle, this is perfect." I smiled at her, "So, let's talk about what comes next," I said, fully expecting this would be my new home. At least for the next 12 months.

We walked back upstairs, "Do you want some coffee or something?" She motioned for me to sit down at the table and waited near the coffee maker for my reply.

I declined and she joined me at the table. "Well, OK. It might sound weird," she hung her head, almost as if in shame.

"What?"

"My fiancé is kind of in law enforcement and we sort of agreed whomever we wanted to move in would have a kind of background check."

"Is that all? That's not a problem. I have a security clearance for my job. You scared me, I thought I was gonna have to do something difficult."

Her bright smile returned, "If you don't mind, can I just have Dave check it out? Then we'll work out some kinda deposit, maybe first and last month's rent? You wouldn't have to pay it all at one time."

"Totally doable," I said with a wave of my hand. "Anything to get out of that outrageous rent at Oakwood."

"Oakwood? Oh my gosh, I hear that place is crazy expensive. How long have you been there?"

Elle and I bonded over a mutual love of John Hughes' movies and all things 80's. She was a spokesperson for a mid-size pharmaceutical company and I could see how. A 31-year old with a Master's in Communication from UVA and B.S. in Chemistry from University of Maryland, she'd settled in D.C. from Bloomington, Indiana. Her fiancé, Dave, was from Chevy Chase and was some kind of investigator or agent in the alphabet soup of D.C.

"Well, you have all of my information, you have the check, talk it over with Dave and let me know," I said as we walked back through the garage.

"Oh gosh, thank you so much for being so great. You have no idea how many people are offended when I mention the background thing," her already high-pitched voice, raised an octave. "I just have to believe this is fate."

I felt the exact same way, "Just lemme know."

"Well, let's assume everything is fine because I already know it is," she smiled, "can you move in by Tuesday?"

"Like this Tuesday?" I was stunned. "That's like two days from now, won't the background thing take longer than that?"

"Nah. Probably not. If you already have a clearance and as long as this doesn't bounce," she playfully waved the check at me and laughed, "I just can't imagine it being a problem.

"Well, what about Lucy?" I remembered the cat even though I'd not seen her during my entire three-hour visit with my new roommate.

"Well, that's kinda my rush." She folded her arms and continued, "I leave Tuesday for three weeks and Dave has this work thing for 10 days and he leaves Wednesday."

"How about this? Call him, see what he says. I mean, I'm good for Tuesday or whenever. You don't have to worry about Lucy or the house being alone or anything. If nothing else, I could help out just while Dave is out of town. Cat sitter, if not roommate," I smiled at her knowing there should be no problem with my clearance or my checking account.

"No, no. This is gonna be fine. I can feel it. Can you come by tomorrow and pick up the key? And hopefully I can introduce you to Lucy. Or rather, introduce Lucy to you." She grinned, "She's a doll and she's really no trouble but for cleaning the liter box which isn't the most pleasant job but god, I would be so grateful."

We agreed to meet after six o'clock. She wasn't sure if Dave would make it but assured me that he wouldn't come over until she got back.

"It's his house, too. I mean, if he wants to come over, I don't mind but it would be kinda awkward if you weren't here."

"No, it's fine. If he can't make it tomorrow, you'll meet him after I get back. Him just showing up here would be too creepy. If it's important to him, he'll make it. But really, if he doesn't show up, it's a sign he trusts you so that might be a good thing." She chuckled, "He's quiet but he really is a sweetheart.

"Well, his fiancée is one of the nicest people I've ever met."

I turned the car around and drove back down the driveway. I could see in my rearview mirror she was smiling and waving as I left. I rolled down my window and gave her a quick wave. I pulled out of the subdivision, lit up a cigarette and wondered if she allowed smoking. I didn't see any ashtrays and the subject hadn't come up. "It probably wouldn't be an entirely bad thing to quit smoking," I said to myself as I took a deep drag of my skinny, menthol cigarette.

I still had a few weeks left on my lease before I had to vacate but decided to go ahead and move out. Lynn said she and the boys would help but since I only had clothes and a few household items, my move went quickly and unassisted.

I called Greg during my first weekend alone.

"Where the hell have you been?" He pretended to scold me then laughed, "Seriously, if not for Lynn telling Ty she saw you at work every day, I woulda thought you fell off the face of the planet."

"It's not like you can't call me," I playfully chided him.

"I know. But hey what's going on?"

I explained to him about the chance meeting I had with Elle and how I'd finally vacated my apartment at Oakwood.

"That's great, that's great. So what else is going on? Gosh, it's good to hear from you," I could almost hear the smile on his face. "Is everything going alright? I mean, everything else, like on a personal level. I've been a little worried about you. Ty said you got jumped in the bathroom at the Westin."

"Oh, that was some bullshit. It didn't get physical or anything like that."

There was silence for a moment, "So, you're not mad at me about that party thing anymore?"

"I owe you an apology about that." I exhaled, "I was totally wrong to react like I did. You were just trying to be a friend and I completely mistook your friendship for interference and that was so wrong. I don't know, I guess that Charlie thing had me all twisted up and I just couldn't see straight. But I see now and I'm sorry."

I heard him swallow hard, "You don't owe me an apology. I'm just glad you're not mad anymore," he paused, "I really have missed you. I've wanted to call you a hundred times."

"Well, now it's me calling you."

And that's how it started. For the next few weeks, Greg and I spent a lot of time together, working out, playing racquetball – which he happily introduced me to at a private club where he was a proud member. We talked for hours while lifting weights or jogging, and made friendly, playful wagers on our racquetball games. Lynn commented on our close friendship asking if there was anything more to it.

"We're friends."

"Well, we miss you. Elizabeth and them are always asking about you." She picked at her salad and continued, "You know, Charlie hasn't been around much either."

"People get busy, I guess," I hoped she didn't notice the curiosity in my voice.

What Lynn didn't know was Ty had called me earlier in the week and specifically asked if I would join them that Friday at the bar. He didn't say exactly what he wanted but I could almost guess it involved a diamond. He swore me to secrecy and asked that I please keep the invitation between us.

"Well, actually, I was thinking about dropping by tomorrow after work for a drink."

"With Greg?" She was openly prying.

I scowled at her, "He's nice and we have a good time together but I'm not dating him."

"Like that would be such a bad thing? You have to admit, he's pretty hot for a white boy," she smiled into her almost empty bowl.

I burst out in laughter, rumpled an unused napkin and threw it at her, "Stop that."

"I'm just sayin'," she shrugged her shoulders then gave me a sardonic smile.

The next day was a blur of phone calls and tracking numbers because an assignment had gotten lost or somehow delayed and might not get to FP&L before the deadline. There were several phone calls to the common carrier, the site-assigned engineer and the drill director. The afternoon ended with Tommy Payton getting on a plane with a copy of the drill documents so he could personally deliver them before midnight, the official deadline.

"Later, kid," he knocked his ring on my desk and left the office with a flash drive and two 3" binders with hard copies of the documents as a backup, "see you Monday."

I heard Lynn click off her desk lamp, "You ready?"

"God, am I. After today I deserve a cocktail. Let me just make sure Tommy's flight is on time so he's not rushing to Dulles for no reason and I'll be right behind you."

"You spoil him, you know that, right?" She smiled at me and playfully rapped her knuckles on my desk as she walked by, "Don't be long, kid."

* * *

It was dark outside so I picked a spot close to one of the lights in the lot at the front of the hotel. I strode through the crisp air and pushed my way through the revolving door. As I swung the door open to the bar, I heard the familiar sound of Ty's laugh and the DJ's almost indiscernible song introduction because his mouth was too close to the microphone. I smiled to myself knowing tonight was going to be memorable.

"Hey, girl!" Elizabeth was the first one to see me.

"Hi, guys," I said to the six or seven people gathered around the table immediately next to the DJ booth.

I greeted everyone then went to the bar to order drinks for myself and those at the table who needed them. Our group swelled to over a dozen people within half-hour. There were some people I didn't know and others I'd seen but never with our group. Everyone laughed and talked. One of the guys brought up hockey causing Elizabeth to roll her eyes and gesturing with her hand while mouthing the words, "blah, blah, blah".

I was having a pleasant evening when out of the corner of my eye, I saw Charlie walk through the side door.

I felt like I was almost holding my breath when one of the men I didn't know told him to grab a drink and join us. I just smiled at Lynn and asked some random question about the newest play Marcus was rehearsing. I could hear her over the music but I wasn't really listening. I was more wondering where Charlie was or where he'd end up. I hadn't seen him since the night his two bottle blonde friends had warned me about staying away from him.

Within a few moments, Charlie was standing behind me. I felt electricity move through my entire body as I heard his voice for the first time in weeks. He spoke to everyone at the table without introductions so that told me he already knew them. It was only a few minutes before Charlie asked the guys if they were interested in "shooting some stick". The men obliged and made their way out of the booth and away from the table. Ty lingered in a kiss with Lynn before he left, giving me a wink and rubbing my shoulder in a friendly, "hang in there" gesture.

I took as many trips as I could to the bar or anything to get a glimpse of Charlie. Since he didn't hesitate to be near me, perhaps time really had been all we needed and we'd be able go on as though nothing ever happened – even our one perfect day. Lynn gave me disapproving looks every time I returned to the table and even one time said, "I know what you're doing." I couldn't help myself. There was something about being close to him that made me want to get closer. Even at the party, when I knew he was furious with me, it was almost like if I just reached out and touched him, the anger would fall away and he'd be the man I knew, not the stranger that had replaced him.

We'd been there for almost three hours and I was seriously considering taking Ty up on his offer to have one of the rooms he'd blocked at a special rate for the night. Now living on the outskirts of Germantown,

I was further from home and the alcohol haze that drifted over me was a concern. I walked out to talk to the front desk when I heard someone behind me.

Before I could wonder who it was, he said, "I need to talk to you." Charlie reached for my arm and walked me vigorously down the long hallway, passing the front desk entirely.

"You can let go of me," I said as he squeezed just above my left elbow and led me outside. The cool air hit me in the face and instantly cleared the buzz I'd been comfortably drifting in, "Where we going?"

"I need to talk to you somewhere private," he quickened his pace, causing me to stumble a bit over the new heels I was wearing special for the occasion. We walked past several rows of cars and toward the back of the parking lot. A shuttle bus parked in the corner seemed to be our destination.

"What's the problem?" I pulled my arm away as we turned the corner on the back of the bus that was parked sideways. As soon as we were on the other side, safely out of sight of anyone in the Westin or its parking lot, Charlie slammed me up against the side of the small bus. I let out a yelp as I hit my head and started to struggle as he pinned my arms to my sides.

"Why are you doing this? Why won't you stop?" He held me against the cold metal as he shouted at me, his face so close to mine I could smell the alcohol on his breath.

"Doing what?" I struggled but he didn't loosen his grip.

"Don't play dumb, it doesn't suit you."

"We had a great day and you blew me off. I just wanted to know why because I liked you and I thought you liked me. I dunno, I just wanted to know what I did that was so wrong." I could feel myself starting to cry and I turned my now aching head to one side hoping he wouldn't see my tears, "Please let me go. I'm sorry. I'm so sorry."

"Please don't cry," he whispered and gently put his mouth on mine. Despite the cold autumn air, his mouth was warm, his lips soft and skilled as I'd remembered.

At first I resisted but eventually began kissing him back, slowly taking his tongue in my mouth. Kissing him felt so good, so natural and I had been thinking about this moment since he left my apartment. It was what I wanted, what I obsessed over for months. He ran his hands around my waist to my back and pulled me to him. It was several minutes before I realized what I was doing. Why was I letting him kiss me? Why was I kissing him? After everything he'd done – even so far as have other women threaten me, how could I even want to be near him? *Don't be stupid.*

I pushed Charlie away and quickly turned to leave. I turned a little too fast for the combination of high heels, alcohol and newly-developing headache, causing me to fall face first into the corner of the bus, hitting my nose and the right side of my face.

Charlie reached for me and asked if I was alright. I pushed his hand away, "Don't fucking touch me!" I steadied myself, holding the rear of the bus and trying to regain my balance. "You know, I don't get you. Why the fuck did you bring me out here? What did you want? You wanna make out with me away from your friends so they wouldn't see that maybe you do like me and I wasn't lying or exaggerating about that Sunday?" I turned around slowly toward him, I could feel myself swaying as I spoke, "And don't you ever put your fucking hands on me again." My whole body trembled, "Just because I choose not to hurt you, doesn't mean I don't know how." It was at that moment I was able to process a familiar pain coming from my face and used the back of my right hand to touch my nostrils, "Fucking great."

Charlie stood there in silence.

I was about halfway to my car on the other side of the parking lot when I realized I didn't have my purse or my keys. I was going to have to go back into the bar. I tried to think of some way I could retrieve my things without having to face my friends but if there was a way, I wasn't able to think of it at that moment. I reached the door to the main building and walked up the same hall Charlie had hustled me down earlier. I tried my best to compose myself so I could walk in, get my things and walk back out. I also knew I needed to get some ice on my face as quickly as possible. The bloody nose probably meant a black eye, maybe two but I knew enough to know my nose wasn't broken – there wasn't nearly enough blood for that. It had been a long time since I had to analyze such injuries but the truth was, I did have experience with such things.

I walked in the bar from the side door having stopped at the ladies' room to try to compose myself. My heart sank when I saw our entire group of friends at the table, Lynn and Ty standing just outside the booth in a tight embrace, people clapping and toasting. I'd missed it.

Lynn was the first one to notice and inadvertently caused the most embarrassing scene possible. "Oh my god, are you alright?" She put her hands on my shoulders and examined another trickle of blood that escaped my nostril. Just over Lynn's shoulder I could see Greg walking to the table with a newly opened bottle of champagne in one hand, his usual Scotch on the rocks in the other. He looked alarmed as he processed what he was seeing.

"I just need my purse, please," I muttered.

"Gimme a napkin," Lynn turned to Ty just as he handed one to her even as she was asking. I took the napkin from her and gently touched my face with it.

"This one?" Viv turned and grabbed the purse she thought was mine that was on the back of the booth between the curved edge and the wall, where we normally left our purses for safe-keeping. There was a look of shock on her face as she slowly handed it to me.

"Thanks," I said before walking out the side door. Lynn and Greg both followed. Just then, Charlie crossed the hall and headed for the front entrance of the hotel. I froze and watched as he walked by, briefly looking up at me then shoving his hands deep in the front pockets of his dark gray trousers and quickened his pace.

That's when Lynn started putting it together. "What did you do?" Her angry voice echoed as she spoke loud enough for Charlie to hear her. He didn't stop or acknowledge Lynn's question.

Once he was out of the building, I started my descent down the side entrance steps when Greg momentarily stopped me, "Wait," he stood in front of me and tried to touch my cheek causing me to flinch, "what happened?" His voice was dulcet and somber. Lynn stood there with us and I could see Ty standing just outside the club watching over the situation.

I made eye contact with him and was only able to manage a tight smile. Looking back at Greg, I mumbled, "It was an accident. I gotta go."

"Lemme walk you to your car," Greg said putting his hand on the middle of my back. I immediately turned my body away and declined the offer.

"No," I snapped. Like a wounded animal, I just wanted to be left alone. I caught myself and tried to adjust my tone, "Really, I'm alright. You guys get back in there. I'll call you." I was looking at Lynn as I spoke, "I'm alright but I gotta go."

I tried to appear strong as I left my friends with a mix of incredulity and sympathy on their faces standing in the lobby. I really didn't need Greg walking me to my car because I wasn't worried about running into Charlie. Even though I didn't know what he meant to do, I knew he didn't mean to hurt me. This was just another unfortunate outcome to an unnecessary confrontation.

Within the space of a few minutes, I had seen the Charlie Diaz I knew, the one I had incredible attraction to and who felt the same about me, and the next, I was confronted with the Charlie Diaz that called me a slut and couldn't even look me in the face.

Whatever this *Dr. Jekyll and Mr. Hyde* thing was, it was the reason he and I couldn't be in the same place at the same time. Ever.

I sat in my car, tears streamed down my face, past the heels of my hands as I pushed them into my eye sockets, willing myself to stop crying. I pulled down my visor and examined my face in the mirror, my brown eyes blurred and red from crying, my right cheek beginning to swell. There was another drop of blood slowly oozing from my nostril,

I patted the droplet with a napkin and flipped up the visor. I knew what the slow-moving blood meant.

"I am so fucking over this," I said to myself as I finally managed to control my crying enough to drive home.

Greg called no less than a dozen times the next day and I eventually turned my phone off. There was only one person that should be calling and I knew he wouldn't. I turned on the phone later in the evening so I could check my voicemail, there was only one.

"Bianca, it's Greg. Please call me. I'm worried about you. I just wanna know you're alright."

I was glad Elle was out of town so I wouldn't have to explain anything to her, at least not for a few days. It was my experience that facial wounds healed quickly so a few days might be all I needed to avoid having the conversation with her.

I wouldn't be so fortunate to avoid the people at work.

When Tommy walked into the office Monday morning, he immediately noticed the bruise under my right eye. "What the hell?" I could tell he was trying to keep a proper tone but his concern got the better of him. The door hadn't even closed before he was at my desk trying to take a closer look, almost as if trying to determine if the injury was caused by an accident or inflicted intentionally.

"It's nothing," I motioned to him with my hand to lower his voice, "don't make a big deal of this."

I saw him glance at Lynn then look back at me, "It's not *nothing*, it's a black eye," he said sitting on the edge of my desk.

"How was Florida? Did you get to FP&L on time? Oh, did you see? Lynn got engaged. Lynn, get over here and show Tommy your – "

"I'll talk to her in a minute, right now I'm talking to you," he threw a look at her and then back to me. He stared into my eyes waiting for me to talk, until finally my phone rang. I was never so happy to hear my office phone. I could deal with a lot of things but the woeful looks from my friends and co-workers was really starting to throw me into a sort of depression. I didn't want anyone to know of the rejection from Charlie, I didn't want them to know that for some reason he thought I was a slut. I didn't want people to see the physical evidence of my inability to handle rejection. It was shameful and shame was a feeling I knew all-too-well and for far too long, and one I'd tried hard for many years to overcome. Or maybe just ignore.

"Why didn't you return any of my calls this weekend?"

I waved at Tom as though this was a call that would take a while. He nodded then walked over to Lynn to congratulate her and ogle the impressive two karat diamond ring she now wore on her left ring finger.

"Is that any way to start a conversation?" I said in a soft voice, trying to make a joke out of what I knew would be a much too serious conversation for my current location.

He was silent on the other end of the line. "Good morning, Bianca. How are you? Why didn't you return any of my calls this weekend? I've been worried about you."

"Thank you." I answered his question in an indirect way, "It's crazy busy here at work. We've got this huge last-minute thing for a utility in Louisiana and I'm gonna be working crazy hours so I might be outta touch for a bit but please believe me, I'm alright. Everything's cool."

I heard Greg exhale deeply, "Bianca, I will find out what happened, either from you or from Charlie."

"Don't you dare!" I shouted into the phone. I quickly looked over to Lynn's desk, gesturing to her I was fine despite my outburst. I hushed and quickly added, "Do not get involved in this. I'm serious. I'm telling you like I'm gonna to tell anyone else who cares about me, don't do or say anything. The best way to help me is to leave it alone. Please. Let's be friends, let's hang out, just not at the Westin."

I could hear the doubt in his voice but when I told him I wanted to have dinner with him after this project he seemed to relax. Although we were working on the last-minute project, it had a Thursday deadline so I would be free after that.

"Will you let me buy you dinner Friday night?" I used the most upbeat tone possible.

"No. But I'll pick you up around seven."

I gently placed the phone back on the receiver and got busy downloading the documents I was going to be working on the next few days.

Lynn tried to ignore the issue but half-way through lunch, she could no longer resist. "Can you please, for once, trust me with something?" She reached across the table with her left hand, touching mine, the simple round diamond of her new engagement ring sparkling on her impeccably manicured hand.

"Lynn, this is such a happy and wonderful time in your life. I'd rather not think about this. Can't we talk about what's going on with you? Are you going anywhere for Christmas vacation? Maybe take Ty to meet your family?" I held her left hand in mine, "Gorgeous ring. It looks beautiful on you. Ty did good. I haven't even congratulated you yet, I'm sorry. I have your gift in my car, I should go – "

"I get it." She squeezed my hand in hers, "You're not gonna tell me. When you're ready, I'm here. And I care. That's all I'll say."

"Thank you." I withdrew my hand from hers and went back to eating my microwave meal, "Now, what's up with vacation?"

We worked 20-hour days so we could finish the project for River Bend by the Thursday deadline. It was after four in the morning when exhausted and in serious need of caffeine, a group of us left the office and headed to the nearest Denny's. Over breakfast, we discussed our plans for the upcoming holiday shutdown.

"I really wish you'd reconsider going with us," Lynn sighed. "Some time away would be good, don't you think?"

"That sounds like a great idea to me, kid." Tommy said taking in a mouthful of coffee then swallowing hard, "You should go."

I shrugged, "If anywhere I'd go to Chicago so I could see my little sister. I haven't seen her since – "

"It's the holidays. Go see your family," one of the other engineers whom I didn't know well interjected, taking a bite of his scrambled eggs, "I'm sure they'd love to see you, especially if it's been a long time like you say."

The lack of sleep and 8th cup of coffee I was drinking made me a dangerous combination of exhausted and grumpy. I almost told him to mind his fucking business but I took a deep breath and tried to remember he meant well.

"Well, I'm gonna get going. I've actually got a date on Friday night," I faked a smile and dropped some cash on the table.

"Get home safe," Lynn said as I pushed through the heavy glass door.

It was the caffeine. It was the stress. It was being over-tired. It was something. Or everything. I couldn't sleep. I kept thinking about what my co-workers said and it got me thinking about something I hadn't wanted to think about in a long time.

I was lonely.

* * *

Dee Dee had invited me over to her sister's place but I declined saying I was busy with work. I hated lying to her but I knew if I told her I just didn't feel like intruding, she'd launch into a whole thing about how I'm not an intrusion and I'm like family. What she couldn't understand was "like family" isn't family. Some things should be reserved for family. I respected that and loved her too much to always tag along. She'd spent the better part of my adult life being like a mother to me and now that we were living our separate lives I was trying not to count on her so much. I still wanted to be friends but I couldn't be one of her kids. Our relationship was evolving and while I sometimes still had the instinct to run crying to her, she was only a three-hour train ride away in New York City, I couldn't do that anymore. I had to handle these things on my own. And I would.

I dove deep into this humiliating obsession but Dee Dee didn't need to know about it. She had her hands full adjusting to life in New York City and her son's new-found fame. The stress of success was real and keeping him grounded was important. She needed to focus on her life, not worry about mine.

I did finally grow tired and one last look at the clock on the nightstand told me I'd only have a couple of hours before I'd have to get up and get back to the office. *"Maybe some time away would be good?"* It was the last thought I had as my heavy eyelids finally fell closed and sleep found me.

* * *

My head was pounding and my eyes stung from lack of sleep, as I rode the elevator instead of taking the single flight of stairs up to my office. I almost never rode the elevator but I was exhausted and the thought of walking a flight of steps when there was a perfectly functioning elevator didn't make any sense. I smiled to myself, a pleasant memory of another time I took an elevator instead of taking a single flight of stairs but the memory quickly left me as I joined the rest of my bleary-eyed co-workers mingling in the kitchen, pouring coffee and comparing notes to see who was most tired. We were all dressed casual, a nice break from our usual business formal attire. Our VP had told us because of how hard we'd worked on the RBS project and with vacation coming up, we were allowed business casual. I was never so grateful not to wear heels.

I was still thinking about that whole "being alone" thing but I couldn't think of anywhere I wanted to go. Chicago was definitely off-limits, especially in the winter. I thought about going back to see a couple of the friends I'd made during my time in L.A. but the truth was, we hadn't kept in touch so to reach out now would probably look pathetic. Besides, those people had families, too. New York was off limits because Dee Dee was in D.C. and I might make time to have lunch or something with her but the point was to go somewhere. I just couldn't think of anywhere that sounded good. No matter where I went, I would be going alone. Why pay money to go be lonely?

That afternoon Greg called. I assumed he was calling to make sure I wasn't going to cancel our dinner date for the next night. I picked up the phone and answered with a sing-song tone in my voice, "This is Bianca. And how may I help you?"

"You have a passport?"

Not exactly what I expected to hear. He explained he was going to San Jose, Costa Rica for a work thing, leaving Sunday, coming back Thursday.

"I can't go to Costa Rica," I saw Lynn's face light up as she walked from the kitchen to my desk. In a barely audible voice she asked, "Is that Greg?"

I nodded my head and gave her the "hush" sign putting my index finger over my lips and scowling at her. She smiled and leaned against the edge of my desk.

"So you don't have a passport?" The tone in his voice was almost condescending.

"I *have* a passport. But you're gonna be working, what am I gonna do?"

Greg explained it was really only a couple of days work at the most but he decided to stay a few extra days to make the trip worth the five-hour flight while still making it back in time to spend Christmas with his family in Atlanta. "It's really more of a one-day thing, probably a dinner but that'd pretty much be it." He went on to explain how he'd never been there and really wanted to share the experience with me, "Unless you can't get the time off work?"

"How much would this little excursion cost?"

"All you need is your airfare, I'll take care of everything else. I mean, the company is taking care of everything, hotel and whatnot."

"So, we'd be staying in the same hotel room?"

"I'm nothing if not a gentleman, Bianca. I'd get a room with two double beds. But we'd be staying in the same room, yes. Unless you want to pay three hundred dollars a night to have a room of your own at the same Marriott."

I forced a laugh, "No. And yes, I know you've always been a perfect gentleman."

"I know how to respect a lady," he sighed and continued, "but you could get a flight for just under six hundred dollars if I book right now."

"Are you serious?" I was about to remark about how inexpensive that sounded to me, "Wait. If *you* book right now?"

"Yeah and that's for the exact same flights I have through our in-house travel department, I don't think you could get this fare calling the airline directly. But it's not a big deal. I just have to pay it and you can pay me back."

I thought about it for a moment, "I can't believe I'm actually considering this." I wasn't sure I wanted to owe someone such a big favor. It wasn't the money, I had money, it was more thinking about "I took you to Costa Rica" being thrown in my face one day.

"Do it," Lynn whispered.

"Can I call you back in like 10 minutes?"

"I know it's short notice but how many chances are you gonna get to go to Costa Rica?" He said with the same excitement I could see in Lynn's eyes.

"I'll call you back." I momentarily sat in silence, looking at the phone before hanging it up. Lynn interrupted my contemplation.

"You have to do it!"

I knew immediately, she was right.

I quickly called Elle and asked about Lucy. She explained that some of her family would be in town that week anyway and that it might actually be perfect timing. "I would never have asked you to leave but if you're going to be out, would you mind if we occasionally used your bathroom? I promise they won't go in your room and whatever they use, I'll replace it."

"Don't be silly. It's your house."

"You pay rent around here and I don't want you to feel uncomfortable in any way."

"Seriously, don't worry. Use whatever or if your guests need it, please feel free. If you want, I can make arrangements to be gone Christmas week."

"Don't you dare, Bee. We're all going to Richmond with Dave's family, kind of a pre-wedding intro thing since our families have never met. We won't be here that week. But if you have plans, I can board Lucy for a few days, no big deal."

"No – no. I'll only be gone a few days next week. I'll be back Thursday, I don't have any plans for the following week. I'll be at the house. Lucy and I will have nachos on Christmas Eve as is my tradition." I was genuinely happy at the thought, "But hey, right now I gotta run and book my plane tickets."

"I'm so jealous!" She snorted in her laughter, "I hope I get to see you before you leave. I feel like I haven't seen you in ages."

I avoided the comment and told her I'd leave a copy of my itinerary on the refrigerator – as was her usual for me. She actually traveled a lot more than I originally expected and I was glad Lucy was a cat and not a dog. It wasn't that she was a lot of trouble but we did spend a lot of time alone together and I had never lived with a dog. I had, however, lived with a cat so I was familiar with their aloof and independent ways.

Elle was always appreciative of me taking care of Lucy and minding the house, she often bought me some small token from wherever she'd visited. I had an entire drawer full of t-shirts and key chains from her travels. She also went out of her way to make a big dinner once a week, usually the kind of home-style cooking I didn't grow up with, meatloaf, pot roast and such, making time to sit down to a meal with me to catch up and tell me, how much she loved having me there. loved having me there.

But she was right, I had been avoiding her and even though the bruise on my face was mostly healed, I'd probably avoid seeing her before I left.

Our flight originated at Dulles, connected through Miami and then non-stop to San Jose. We arrived just before 7 P.M. local time and took a short shuttle bus ride to the Marriott. I was surprised by all of the familiar franchises there – McDonald's, Tony Roma's, even Kentucky Fried Chicken. It wasn't at all what I'd expected. I guess I wasn't exactly "continental".

The real surprise came when we arrived to the hotel. It was set on an old coffee plantation. The open air lobby was flanked on either side by clay water fountains. Just down the open corridor was a courtyard, a group of three men sat rolling handmade cigars. Elaborately painted green and blue tile complimented the sunny yellow walls. It was the most beautiful hotel lobby I'd ever seen.

"This is amazing," I commented when we got to our second floor accomodations. There were two queen size beds on one side of the room, with a large, shuttered window on the adjacent wall that opened to a spectacular view of the grounds. In the corner sat a large wing-backed chair with a matching ottoman. The third wall featured a low, four-drawer dresser and a flat panel TV mounted directly onto the wall.

"I'm glad you like it," Greg's voice was flat.

"Don't you?" I asked spinning around to try to read his face.

"It's nice," he sounded nonplussed.

"Oh come on, it's gorgeous. I'm so glad you invited me," I walked over to him, reached up on my tip-toes and kissed his cheek.

He smiled at me and touched my hair as I stood in front of him, "I don't know that I've ever seen you this happy."

"Well, I haven't been this happy in a long time." I turned around, "But I mean, look at this place," I walked back to the window and looked out, "it's incredible."

Greg joined me and drew in a deep breath.

"You alright?" I asked touching his shoulder and starting to think something was off.

"Just a little jetlag maybe," he forced a smile at me then continued looking out the window.

"Why not take a shower and let's go do something?"

"Let me get the work stuff outta the way then we'll plan something fun, OK?" The solemn tone in his voice embarrassed me, I'd almost forgotten about the work stress he must be under.

"I'm so sorry. You're right." I walked away from the window and over to where my stroller bag sat, collecting my thoughts and trying to figure out how to make up for my selfishness. "How about this? Why don't you take a shower, I'll unpack our stuff and get us some room service?"

He turned to me and smiled a sincere, warm smile this time, "That is an excellent idea." He took a quick look at the menu and left me so he could unwind in a long, hot shower. I was happy he trusted me to organize his things into the drawers and closet. It had been a long time since I took care of anything for a man that wasn't my boss.

We enjoyed our quiet evening. I was reading one of the newest books from my favorite author of crime drama while Greg worked furiously on his laptop. We left the windows and shutters open most of the evening until cigar smoke wafted up from the courtyard below giving Greg a headache. "I have to close these," he said with a touch of frustration in his voice. I was half-asleep and didn't care one way or the other. Either the smoke had awoken him or he was still awake working as I slept off my jetlag.

Early the next morning, Greg woke me with a gentle touch and a whisper to advise that he'd be back as quickly as he could. "They eat lunch really late down here, so I'm thinking I should be freed up after that, probably two o'clock or somewhere around there. Do whatever you want, just please don't leave the hotel."

"No problem," I answered with a throaty, sleep-drenched voice. "I'll be right here waiting when you get back."

He smiled and kissed my forehead. I rolled over and went back to sleep.

Breakfast was over by the time I woke up and I decided I'd wait until lunchtime to eat anything. I contemplated what to do but since Greg specifically asked me not to leave the hotel, I figured about the only thing I could do was hang out by the pool.

I changed into a modest, one-piece swimsuit that had an aqua and white print with a matching sarong. I occasionally took a dip in the water but mostly spent my time reading and enjoying the warm sun. With my eyes closed, lounging on a teak chaise, I could hear soft music sung in Spanish. The exquisite, delicate melody was a betrayal to the pain in the lyrics, a misrepresentation of the songwriter's stanzas about lost love. If you knew the language and paid attention to the words, you'd know the music was a cunning mask for the grief and regret that the ballad was really about.

I was out for a few hours, mindful to put sunscreen on each time I got out of the pool. It had been years since I'd had sunburn but I remembered how miserable and painful it was.

I returned to the room, took a shower and ordered some lunch. I made sure to pay for the room service with cash I'd changed at the airport. I didn't want Greg to get in trouble for extraneous charges. During lunch, I felt a slight stinging sensation on my nose and cheeks. After I finished the last bites of the sandwich that wasn't exactly the kind of turkey club sandwich I was used to, I tended to the beginnings of mild over-exposure to sun. I gently patted aloe vera gel onto the bridge of my nose and cheeks, the pink flesh getting more pink by the minute.

I was wearing one of the white bathrobes provided by the hotel when I dropped into the chair and put my feet up on the ottoman, turning my face away from the window enjoying the light breeze on my neck. I knew I should get up and dress but I couldn't motivate myself to move. Instead, I drifted off to sleep and thought, "I guess I did need a vacation."

I awoke to the sound of the shower running. The television was turned on but the volume down. The combination of sun and sleep had left me a bit disoriented for a moment until I realized where I was. I slowly got up from the chair, retied my robe and walked to the bathroom, knocking on the door loud enough for Greg to hear me over the sound of the shower.

"Hey, sweetness," Greg called.

"How was it?"

"You can come in," he shouted so I could hear him, "I'm just in the shower." Greg peaked his head out from behind the opaque white shower curtain as I walked into the small, steamy room, "I see you got some sun."

"Yeah. I did," I touched my cheek. "So, it went well today?"

"Yes. So well, I'm done already."

"I thought you were gonna have a dinner or something? Does this mean we have to go back sooner than you expected?" I was trying not to sound disappointed.

"Not at all. Just means I don't have to worry about work the rest of the trip." He turned off the shower, "Well, I do have a couple of things I have to get done and it'll make me look busier than I actually am but since there is someone back home monitoring what I'm doing I do kinda wanna look busy. But that doesn't mean we can't do anything fun. I just have to make sure I'm on the VPN from time-to-time." I could see he was shaking excess water off of his hair that was longer these days than he usually wore it.

"I'll give you some privacy," I left the bathroom and took a seat on the chair where I'd just napped. I started thinking about Greg. Lynn was right. He had a great smile and gorgeous dark blue eyes that was an interesting combination with his dark blonde, almost brown hair. He was athletic and liked to do a lot of the same things I did, why had I never thought about him in a romantic way? Had I not noticed? He was sweet and seemed to always be there for me, why would I have dismissed such a great guy? Here I was taking so much time and energy agonizing over the Charlie Diaz thing when I had a perfectly wonderful guy right here. Here, in this beautiful place, in this very hotel room. A guy that cares about me so much, he invited me to Costa Rica with him. No strings. No promises. No expectations.

As if on cue, Greg walked out of the bathroom wearing nothing but a towel. His upper body glistened with water and his just-above-the-shoulder hair dripped water at the ends that ran down his smooth chest. "So, what do you wanna do tonight?" He used the towel from around his shoulders to frantically rub his wet head.

What I really wanted to do was slink over to him, unwrap his towel and take him to bed. It was as if all of a sudden I wasn't seeing my friend but a lover. Maybe more.

I smiled at him but said nothing.

"What are you thinking?" A smile snuck across his lips as though he might be reading my thoughts by the look on my face.

I started fantasizing about the seduction. How I'd walk over to him and without saying a word reach my hand into his towel, kiss his chest and explore his stiffening manhood with my hand, stroking his growing shaft then move my mouth to his. With my other hand, untie my robe and let it fall to the floor.

"Bianca?" Greg said waving his hand in front of my face.

I realized I'd just been holding my breath and I exhaled. "Um, I don't know. You decide." I suddenly felt the blush of arousal.

"I would love to know what you were just thinking," he said smiling and bending down to put his face near mine.

"I'm sure you would," I said standing up. "Do you mind if I take a shower while you decide what you wanna do?"

"Be my guest," he said making a sweeping gesture with his hand. "I'm thinking dinner before anything. I'm kinda hungry."

"Sure," I said, starting to untie my robe and let it slip from my shoulder before I was in the bathroom, giving Greg a hint of what I was thinking. I took my time in the shower, making sure to touch up my bikini area thinking maybe for the first time in a long time there was actually a reason to care about such things.

We left the room around seven o'clock to dinner but to my surprise, there weren't many people at the restaurant in the hotel. Greg explained that dinner is also eaten much later in the evening than is custom in the U.S., more like nine or even ten o'clock at night.

We sat across from each other on the veranda at a glass and wrought iron table with cushions on both the seat and backs of the chairs making it very comfortable. The light breeze felt good and gently blew Greg's hair. He looked deep into my eyes but didn't say a word. He just sipped his Scotch, never breaking his gaze. "You know, I've been attracted to you for a very long time," he took a sip, the dark gold liquid barely touching his lips, "ever since the first time I met you at Corbin's house."

"That was a couple years ago but I remember meeting you the first time I came to D.C." I bit the inside of my bottom lip, "If I remember correctly, you had a girlfriend at the time."

"Yeah." This time he took a stiff swig, "Well, I remember meeting you and thinking you were very beautiful." He put his glass down, "I think you're even more beautiful now."

We slowly and quietly worked through dinner. I was sure we both knew what we'd be doing once we got back to the room. It was like we each wanted to savor the moments leading up to our first kiss and our first time together.

Although it was almost painful waiting for the check, I knew it had to be done this way. I couldn't rush this. After dinner, we casually strolled the grounds, hand-in-hand, taking time to digest our food before going back to the room although neither of us had eaten very much of the fish entrées we'd ordered.

When we got to the room, I casually undressed, careful not to reveal too much too fast but I didn't hide my body from him. He stood in the doorway of the bathroom undressing, watching as I brushed my teeth. As I exited the bathroom wearing only my pale pink bra and matching panties, he gently palmed my stomach with his hand, "I'll be right out."

I heard him in the bathroom brushing his teeth. I could hardly think what I should do. Should I lie on the bed? Continue standing?

The window.

I made sure it was closed so as not to disturb us later when the inevitable scent of cigar smoke would make its way to our room. I was closing the shutters when Greg walked up behind me, his arms snuck around my waist and pulled me to him. I happily sank into his long chest.

"Giving everyone a show?" He kissed my ear.

He turned me around slowly, his hand holding my cheek, and moving his mouth to mine. My mouth immediately opened to accept his tongue when his lips touched mine. His hands ran up my back and pulled me closer. He slowly withdrew his tongue from my mouth and pulled away from me, one arm still wrapped around me, he put his hand on my cheek and brushed his thumb over the barely visible bruise under my eye. I could feel the erection in his pajama bottoms straining against the fabric and into my belly.

"Bianca, before we go any further, we have to talk. Maybe you should put something on," he went to the closet and brought me the bathrobe I'd worn earlier.

I immediately felt self-conscious about my arousal. I put the robe on and sat on the corner of the bed I'd slept in the night before, "Is everything alright?"

He pulled a t-shirt over his head and sat on the ottoman, "I never thought we'd ever be this – close." Now, he seemed embarrassed by his arousal. He looked down at his hands and continued, "I've been trying to figure out how to tell you this. Well actually, I've wanted to tell you many times and I've been trying to work up the courage ever since we were on the plane coming here but I –"

"Just say it," I was panicking, "You're kinda freakin' me out."

"I never wanted this to happen. I mean, I wanted *this* to happen," he said looking around the room, "but I didn't want any of this to get to this point."

"Greg, just say it," I had no idea what he was talking about but suddenly felt I would spontaneously combust if he didn't give me an explanation.

"Charlie."

I felt the blood rush out of my head, "What does he have to do with anything?"

"I…"

"What the fuck. Just tell me. Geezus." I couldn't help it, I was starting to feel angry even though I had no idea what it was about. The fact it had to do with Charlie Diaz infuriated me, "What – is – it?"

"When you and Charlie had that one date, that one Sunday," he drew a deep breath, "he told me all about it on Monday at work and I was shocked. I mean, I've known you longer and you never even looked in my direction but you meet him and then in one day it's like you're already a couple."

"What did you do?" I asked quietly.

"I just want you to understand…"

"What did you do?" I yelled. I tried to regain my composure but still projecting anger with my tone, "Just tell me what you did." I was starting to get a picture in my mind but I needed him to tell me exactly what he needed to confess.

"I told Charlie you and I slept together."

"What? Why?"

"Because I'm a jealous dick. I told him we'd slept together knowing he wouldn't go out with you again if he knew you and I had a thing."

"That's why he thinks I'm a slut?"

He sighed, "I made it seem like we were sleeping together even when you were pursuing him."

"I wasn't pursuing him, I was trying to understand why he hated me so much. Geezus, Greg. Why would you do this?"

"Look, I could have slept with you but I didn't. So, as much as you wanna hate me right now, at least I told you this before I fucked you."

"Don't you dare! Don't you fucking dare try to make yourself feel better about this," I was starting to feel sick. I had to get out of there. I wasn't sure what I was going to do but I knew it wasn't going to be in that room with Greg Schicker.

"I'm sorry," he stood up after I grabbed my bag from the closet. "Just don't go right now, it's late."

"You have no idea what you've done," my heart was pounding in my chest as I methodically searched the room for my things.

"I do know."

"You must really hate me," I announced as I packed the last of my clothes.

"I don't hate you," he said walking behind me.

I turned and pushed him out of my way as I stomped to the bathroom to collect my toiletries.

I zipped the black carry-on closed and was about to drop it to the floor, "What else, Greg?"

"Bianca, please. Don't do this," he held his hands flat across the top, trying to keep the bag on the bed.

"Get away from me. I'm serious." I ripped off my robe and stepped into the dress I'd left on the bed, "I'm leaving and you can just go fuck yourself."

"Please don't do this. I'll tell you everything, just don't go."

"Oh, there's more? Great." I stared daggers at him, "I don't fucking believe you. You could've done this back in Maryland. But no." I shook my head, "You wait until we're in another fucking country."

"I told Charlie we'd slept together."

"You told him you fucked me."

"OK yes, I told him I fucked you. More than once." He exhaled, "And I took him to the card party because I knew how upset you were about the whole thing and Charlie was starting to think about having a conversation with you to tell you why he wasn't interested in pursuing anything with you so I took him to the party and told him you and I had fucked earlier that night."

"Nice, I firmly took the bag off the bed and inadvertently let it fall a bit too hard onto the floor.

"Aren't we a couple of idiots?" I huffed and started to the door.

"You're not an idiot," he said quietly.

"No, you're a fucking asshole."

"I know," he sat on the bed.

"I just couldn't believe you guys were so hot and heavy after knowing each other for like one day. You never looked at me the way you did him. Not until tonight anyway," he clasped his fingers and held them in his lap.

"Honestly, and this is the funniest part, I always kinda thought you were full of shit. Stupid me, I trusted you anyway."

"It's not your fault. I mean, I was just being a jealous prick and I'm sorry. But Charlie – "

"I'm not gonna talk about him with you." I opened the door and rolled my bag out behind me, "Just once I thought I could have a relationship with someone where only he and I were involved."

"It's not a good idea for you to be going around by yourself," I heard him say as the door closed.

I heard the door open again, "Bianca, I had no idea he'd ever hit you."

I stopped for a moment and turned to face him, "You don't even know what the hell you're talking about." I shook my head, "And you think a bruise on my face is more hurtful than this?" I turned back around and proceeded to the front desk. The clerk asked if I really wanted to leave at such a late hour, "Miss, I can get you a room here for the night and you can leave in the morning." Even through his thick accent, I could hear the concern in his voice.

I saw Greg still dressed in pajama pants and t-shirt, looking down at me from the open staircase. I immediately switched over to Spanish knowing Greg, if he could hear, wouldn't be able to understand anything I was saying. The gentleman behind the desk seemed surprised that I was fluent, "As long as there are flights out tonight, I'm going."

He nodded and called for the shuttle driver.

I arrived at the airport and proceeded immediately to the local airlines' counter and asked for the next flight out. The agent told me the next and last flight out for the night was to San Salvador.

"That's El Salvador, Miss."

"I know," I smiled at her, "that's perfect." I handed her my credit card and passport.

I had never been to San Salvador and hadn't expected to be going to San Salvador so I was at a total loss as to where I'd stay. All I knew was it was the capital city of El Salvador and therefore should have any number of hotels. I struck up a conversation with one of the flight attendants on my half-full flight and asked if she could recommend a place. She said the crew usually stayed at one of the Marriott's.

"Fine by me," I nodded.

I asked if there was a shuttle bus to the property or if I should take a taxi. She explained that while there was a shuttle, at that time of night it was best to take a taxi. I was grateful for the insight and hailed a cab as soon as I hit the curb at Comalapa International. It was well after midnight before I got to my room. I unpacked, took a hot shower and applied more aloe to the now stinging sunburn on my face. I climbed into bed, mentally exhausted. I didn't wake up until well after noon the next day.

The Marriott my flight attended had recommended was pleasant but not nearly as spectacular as the San Jose property I'd stayed in the night before. It didn't have the charm or views of the old coffee plantation but it was still nice and the bed was very comfortable, although for some reason I was stiff and groggy as though I hadn't slept well. Even in my fog, I was strangely optimistic.

It hadn't been my fault after all.

But then again, maybe it was. How did I not see this coming? Why didn't I listen to my good judgment? I knew there was a reason Greg always seemed off-limits to me and it was more than the fact that he had a girlfriend the first time I met him. It was my good sense telling me to stay away. The good sense I once again ignored. I growled and rolled over, I had no desire to face the day. I just wanted to get some rest. Maybe now I *could* rest. I could rest knowing I couldn't do anything. I didn't ruin anything. I lay on my side, my right hand under a pillow, my left resting on top of it. Seeing the faint scar that ran down the middle of my left wrist, *"I'm not a slut,"* I whispered to myself then drifted back to sleep. I didn't look at the clock again until dusk, when my stomach growled and hunger no longer let me sleep. It had been almost 24 hours since my last meal. My final meal with Greg Schicker.

I showered and decided to venture down to one of the two restaurants on the property and see what might look good. It made me a little nervous when I saw guards with automatic weapons and energetic German Shepards on leashes patrolling the perimeter of the hotel so I decided not to take dinner outside but rather sit inside and not draw so much attention to the fact that I was there alone.

The place was practically empty so I had my choice of where I wanted to be, on the patio, in the dining room or at the bar. Where I really wanted to be was home with Lucy, snuggling on the sofa with a fire cracking while reading a book – but that was not to be. Even if I did go home, I'd have nothing to go home to. I'd promised Elle that I'd be gone until Thursday, just enough time for her and her family to vacate. No, I was in Central America, even if it wasn't Costa Rica, until Thursday.

I walked through the dining room, telling the host I preferred to take dinner in the bar. He smiled and gestured an approval.

* * *

I noticed Ian right away. His silky blonde hair moved with the breeze of the ceiling fans several feet above his bar stool. We smiled at each other as I walked by and took a seat on the far side of the bar from him. Before I even ordered my first drink, he moved over a couple of stools and introduced himself. He explained he was in El Salvador on his way back from a trade show in Buenos Aires. He said he worked for a company based in Germany but was from Holland.

"And what's your name?" He asked in a thick, Dutch accent.

"Bianca." I was surprised at how immediately I answered.

"Good to meet you, Bianca. Ian Uwe Houwezinka. But you can just call me Ian, as I will just call you Bianca." He shook my hand, "You here on business?" He motioned to the bartender for another drink, "You want another?"

"No, thank you," I pointed to the almost completely full vodka tonic the bartender had sat in front of me a moment earlier.

"So, you didn't answer."

"I'm just on my way from Costa Rica," I took a sip of my beverage.

"Ahhhh," he said with an exaggerated tone, "but you speak the language, right?"

"What makes you say that?" I was curious how he would know since I hadn't spoken any Spanish yet.

"Well, most women your age wouldn't come to a country alone without knowing the language."

"My age?" I jokingly tried to sound insulted and we smiled at each other.

His astute observation told me he was a frequent traveler. Within an hour, I learned Ian was happily married with two children. He hated the extensive travel required for his job and took a lot of pride in his family. He had several photos of each child and several more of just his wife.

"That's so nice," I examined the photos not genuinely interested but still caring enough to fake it for the friendly stranger.

We talked about his job, his friends, and various world events. I was impressed with his worldliness and great command of English and Spanish, neither his native language. He looked like he might be close to 35 – maybe 40, but proved me wrong by saying he'd been married for 27 years.

"You're kidding me. Ian, how old are you?"

"I'm 52 this year," he said proudly.

"You look much younger than that."

"It's all the clean living," he said raising a half-full Jack Daniels and Coke.

I gestured for a toast, "To clean living."

We'd been at the bar almost three hours, talking and catching up as if we were old friends. When Ian asked me to join him for dinner, it didn't surprise me how fast I accepted. He flagged down a waiter, telling him we'd like to move to a table.

During the unnecessarily long wait for menus, I excused myself and went to the ladies' room. Once there, I examined myself in the mirror, "See, you're alright. Everything's fine." I forced a smile to my own reflection just to see how it looked to the rest of the world. I was always good at faking a smile.

I returned to the table and found Ian had not only gotten menus but another round of drinks. I sat down quietly, not interrupting his review of the menu. I started to pick up my glass but then set it back down.

"I took the liberty of getting you another drink," he didn't look up as he spoke.

I thanked him then asked, "So, see anything good?"

"Everything here is good. Especially seafood. Seriously."

I looked at the newly filled rock glass sitting in front of me. I picked it up and examined it, "Damn. There's something floating in this." I looked around before pushing my chair back, "I'm gonna go get a new drink, I'll be right back."

Ian looked at me over the reading glasses that sat well below the bridge of his nose, "Sure."

I returned with a new drink in my hand and sat down, picking up the menu, "So, did you decide on something?"

"Not a very trusting person, are you?" Ian put his menu down and smiled.

"I'm a very trusting person, actually. I mean, we just met and I've told you my whole life story. Or as much as you can say over the course of a couple of hours."

"Actually," he grinned, set his forearms on the table and leaned on them, "I've done most of the talking." He looked down at my drink, "And you replaced the drink I ordered you."

Another astute observation.

He took his glasses off, "You're a paradox, Bianca."

"Not really," I continued to review the menu and didn't look at him even though I knew he was looking at me.

"Ah, but you are."

Just then, the waiter appeared and took our order.

"So what really happened? Why are you in San Salvador?"

"I told you, I went to Costa Rica with a friend. He's there for work so I decided to take a quick jaunt somewhere else. You know, just experience what I can while I'm down in this part of the world. I don't have a cool job like yours." I threw him a bashful grin and hoped he'd drop the subject.

"No one leaves Costa Rica for El Salvador. It's like leaving San Diego to go to Detroit." He took a swig of his drink, "I've had good fun in Detroit but given the chance to visit one or the other, I'd pick San Diego."

I suddenly felt guilty for lying by omission, "It's a long story."

"We have time. As you've noticed, the service here is really slow," he laughed a hardy laugh then waited for me to start talking.

"It's true. I went with a friend to Costa Rica. He's there on business. So while we're there, we have a fight. I decide I don't wanna stay there with him so I decide to take a side trip until my return flight on Thursday."

"So, you just jumped on a plane to anywhere?"

"I suppose you can say that."

"That's probably not very safe or very smart, Bianca."

"Well, I figure I know the language and I've traveled around on my own. I mean, I'm used to doing everything alone anyway." I shrugged, "Plus, I'm comfortable among strangers."

"Um-hm."

"What?" I asked, referring to his quiet, judgmental tone.

"It's just interesting. Like I said, you're a paradox."

"How's that?"

"You're not only comfortable with strangers, you *prefer* them."

"I like to meet new people."

"No," he shook his head. "Take me for example. You figure this is a purely ephemeral meeting, so you're not afraid to open up to me. I can't hurt you because I'll never see you again."

"I'm not afraid of people. I'm only afraid of people who say I love you." I was surprised at my admission. I could see by the look on Ian's face, he was too but I continued, "I can basically handle just about anything but someone saying they love me."

"Why?" He looked puzzled.

"It's not really important, is it?"

"To me? I don't know. But it should be important to you."

I decided that I'd explain the recent situation with Charlie and Greg from the very beginning.

We finished dinner and sat sipping espresso.

I worried that I'd shared too much. I liked Ian. I respected him. I wanted him to respect me. I didn't want him to see me as damaged. I wanted him to see my strength.

It was well past one o'clock in the morning when the bartender alerted us for last call. Ian and I continued talking, touching on less-sensitive subjects and drifting back to Charlie and Greg. Ian's question was my own, *"Why did Charlie react so violently?"*

"I don't know. I guess I deserved it. I mean, I had no idea what had happened and I suppose my constantly asking what was wrong drove him crazy."

"Or maybe he was already a little off? It might be better things didn't work out with someone like that. Who knows what you might have been in for?"

"I don't believe that for a minute. I really just think he thought I was fucking with him. But I can't really answer that. I don't know, I just know I wasn't ever afraid of him."

"Good on you, woman," he said almost disgusted, "I might have to kick his ass if I ever met him."

"Aren't you glad you're happily married?"

"Ah, I'm very happily married but it doesn't mean I don't understand."

He reached over and patted my hand in a fatherly way, "You will be fine."

"I know."

As I reached for the check and insisted to pay, Ian quickly snatched the small leather portfolio from my hand, "Pardon, I know we Dutch have a certain reputation but I don't allow a lady to pay the check."

I briefly struggled with him in a playful way, "Can I at least leave the tip?"

"No," he said placing his credit card in the plastic sleeve and closing the portfolio, "I'm happy to do it."

A while later when we finally got up, I asked Ian when he'd be leaving.

He looked at his watch, "Roughly ten hours from now. I have to take a run up to Mexico City, then finally back home."

"Well, I had a good evening. Thank you for everything."

"Thank you for the company," he said shaking my hand.

"Yeah, you've got a great story for your wife. The crazy American girl with the shitty luck with men."

"No," he shook his head, "the really intelligent American woman who kept me great company in San Salvador."

"Well, thank you," I bowed my head and accepted the compliment.

He gave me his business card and asked me to stay in touch, "And when you get back home, send me your résumé. I would love to have someone that could cover this part of the world for me. I'm getting too old." He ran his fingers through his thin blonde hair, "I think you could be great at this job."

"I don't know anything about sales. I'm an admin. Although I'm also an FTD-certified florist, if that helps," I smirked.

"You know people, you know the language and you're not afraid to travel. The other stuff you can learn."

"Well, I'll keep that in mind," I said with a half-laugh.

"Seriously, keep in touch. Let me know what happens with this Charlie thing."

I nodded and started to walk toward the elevator.

"Wait," Ian blurted, "I just want to say this one thing." He walked closer to me, "I know you don't love this Charlie guy. And you don't love Greg either. But somewhere along the line you did love someone. It's why you're so afraid of allowing yourself to feel it or even think about it. So whomever it was that hurt you, whether it was a lover or your mother, it doesn't matter who it was – you have to let go of the hurt. Even if you don't forgive them, at least do right by yourself and let go of the hurt." He spoke with such sincerity, "I've only known you a few hours and I can see you cling to that hurt like a safety net, a way to keep people away from you. And you think if you don't love anyone you can't get hurt. Well, after this business with Charlie, you know that's not true." He drew a breath, "Love isn't the burden, Bianca. The pain you're holding onto is."

"I'll be in touch," I said, shaking his hand again, not even sure if I meant it. "Good night."

"Be well," he said as I activated the elevator with my room key card and watched the doors close.

I woke up the next morning to the room service I'd preordered, the knock at the door jarring me out of sleep just after nine o'clock. I sat down to drink my fresh coffee and nibble on some wheat toast and noticed the flashing light on my hotel room phone. I called down to the front desk and was informed it was a voice mail system and was told how to access messages.

It was Ian.

"Bianca, it was so nice meeting you and I'm serious about sending me your résumé. But really I called to say good bye and ask you to please call your friend and let him know where you are. I'm sure he's crazy with worry right now. No matter how mad you are, don't do that to him. Take care of yourself."

I listened to the message several times before deleting it. I knew he was right.

After breakfast, I called downstairs and asked if they could look up the phone number to the Marriott in San Jose. The front desk rang me through within seconds of putting me on hold. I got the operator to transfer me directly to the room's voicemail so I could leave a message. I left word for Greg that I'd be staying in El Salvador for the duration and only going back to San Jose so I could take the flight back to the States. And although I told him I was in San Salvador, I didn't tell him where I was staying.

I spent the next day doing everything I could to keep from thinking about my inevitable next meeting with Greg. I spent a lot of my time by the pool, in the shade this time, reading a book. I decided there was no way I would be lucky enough to meet another "Ian" so I ordered in and surfed the unusually large channel lineup on the hotel's cable system. Greg Schicker wasn't ever far from my mind and neither was Charlie Diaz.

And, as ever, neither was Jeff Syddall.

As I packed my things that night, I felt an anger welling up from deep inside of me. An anger bordering on rage. What would I say? What could I say? Greg wouldn't care one way or the other. The fact that he was capable of this kind of manipulation told me everything I needed to know. No amount of words, no matter how harsh, would ever make him feel the way he made me feel. How could he have done this to me? How could I have been so stupid as to believe him? I knew from the first time I met Greg he was full of shit, how did he fool me? My defenses were up. I thought I was sharp. I thought back to Charlie's verbal assault at the party and his fury in the parking lot of the Westin. I quickly stood up and gathered my travel documents.

"There's no fucking way I'm getting on the same flight as Schicker," I mumbled to myself and called the airline.

I found I could take an early flight back to Miami and even a different flight back to D.C. if I wanted to pay the fees and fare difference.

"I'll pay it," I told the very patient call-center agent who was doing her best to accommodate my requests. I could hear her fingers flying over her computer keyboard, "Please just get me on those flights."

I felt better that I'd changed my plans. Relieved. I knew I was still going to have to face Greg but I wouldn't have to sit next to him on a plane for five hours. I was restless and I couldn't sleep. I felt myself squeezing my eyes closed willing myself to drift off. I attributed the insomnia to all the sleep I'd gotten in recent days but the truth was I was anxious about seeing Greg and wondering how I would handle someone who had manipulated my life so subtly yet so deeply, with a cruelty I'd not known in a very long time.

I'm fragile. I know it. I can almost feel my heart break into a thousand pieces from a harsh word. But like a tiny shard of glass carelessly left on the kitchen floor, I can inflict a sudden and shocking amount of pain when it's least expected. Charlie didn't know me. Greg didn't know me. They couldn't imagine the kind of hurt I could cause them if I would so choose. I was trying not to use my uncanny ability to read people and use words as weapons. I was trying not to wound people by using their insecurities against them. I was trying not to use the blunt tools I'd acquired from a painful childhood to exact a kind of revenge on those that hurt me. But the thought of telling Greg he's a heartless sociopath with nothing going for him but good looks that will eventually betray him and leave him with nothing but a grotesque *Dorian Gray* legacy of regret actually made me smile. I relished the thought of telling him that even a gold-digger from Arkansas realized she could do better than him. Alas, I'd only know when he was actually in front of me what I'd say and how brutal I'd choose to be to him.

I gazed out the window during my short flight to San Jose, trying to imagine the conversation I'd have with Greg. What I'd say, what he'd say and if any amount of words would ever make him sorry for what he did. I wondered if he was wondering about me. Was he worried? Was he as anxious about seeing me as I was about seeing him?

It felt like it took forever to get through Immigration and Customs, not the experience I remembered from the first time I was in Costa Rica a couple of days earlier. By the time I was in line for a taxi, I was in a full-blown panic. What if Greg had decided to leave? What if he said "fuck it" and went back to D.C. without me? When we arrived back to the hotel, I jumped out of the car and impatiently waited for my cab driver to open the trunk. I handed him fare and a huge tip, then rushed to the front desk, "Can you please ring Greg Schicker's room for me?"

I thought I was going to faint when the lady behind the desk told me he'd already checked out. I could feel my mouth hanging open, my mind racing, wondering what I'd do next. I already had my reservations and I knew I was going back to the airport shortly but for some reason my mind went blank and I suddenly had no idea what to do.

I stared blankly at the clerk when I felt a hand on my shoulder.

"Hi," Greg said, his rolling luggage bag next to him, "I've been waiting for you."

"Hi," I know he heard the relief in my voice.

"I wasn't gonna leave without you," he turned toward the courtyard and pointed to an area with tables and wicker furniture. "You wanna have a seat over here?" He started walking that direction.

"I won't be flying back with you," I said following him.

"What?" He stopped briefly, then continued to the table.

"I actually don't have a lot of time. I'm taking an earlier flight."

"I understand," he said pointing to a table and waiting for me to be seated before he sat down.

We were quiet for several minutes until I broke the silence, "I'm sorry I left the way I did."

"God, Bianca. I was so worried. I would never forgive myself if something happened to you."

I bit my tongue and tried not to come out swinging. "That's why I called and left a message," I said in a tight voice.

"I was relieved to hear you were alright. I didn't think you'd go home but I wasn't sure. And I wasn't looking forward to calling your house and having Elle freak out."

"I won't pretend that I handled things the best possible way. I guess when it comes to fight or flight, I literally choose flight." I laughed at myself.

"You were justified," Greg hung his head and picked imaginary dirt from under his fingernails.

"Look at me for a minute," I said, reaching out for his hand so he'd stop fidgeting, "I am so, so sorry if I did anything to hurt you. That includes a few days ago. And I do appreciate you telling me what you'd done before we fucked." I let go of his hand and continued, "It doesn't relieve your responsibility but Charlie didn't have to react the way he did."

"I'm sorry about that, I really had no idea – "

I stopped him, "Just let me finish." I put my hand up as if to physically stop him.

"OK," he said leaning back in his chair.

"Was any of it real?" I had no idea why I asked the question but found myself holding my breath as I waited for the answer.

Greg ran his fingers through his hair, "Bianca..." his voice trailed off and he sat quietly, folding then unfolding his hands.

"I just wanna know the truth," I managed to force the words out of my throat in barely a whisper.

"Maybe not in the beginning," he stopped himself and looked at me, his eyes were dull and he looked as though he hadn't slept in days. We just stared at each other for a moment until the silence became unbearable.

I decided to stop the pain, "So, thanks for inviting me." I changed the tone in my voice and tried to sound strong, "I probably would've never had a chance to see Central America and it's quite beautiful."

In my mind there had been so much to say. Call him a bastard, tell him to fuck himself, call him a miserable, awful person that should be ashamed of himself but I just couldn't bring myself to do it. It was as if I was so hurt, all I could do was pretend not to be.

But there was one thing I knew I had to make clear.

"Greg, I'm gonna make a promise to you and you're gonna make a promise to me." My tone remained strong and I sat completely upright and tossed my bangs to the side with a flip of my head, "Now, you know we're not gonna be friends after this, there's just no way. But I'm going to make this promise, not even so much for your sake but for my own. I'd rather not have people know how you have completely humiliated me."

Greg huffed, shifted in his seat and re-crossed his legs, he seemed annoyed, as if I was going to impose on him.

"So, I promise neither Diane nor Dr. Chapman or any of that group of our friends will ever hear about this from me."

He exhaled as if he'd forgotten I knew people in his life that didn't go to the bar at the Westin. "And what do I need to promise you?" His tone was almost one of mocking.

I sat forward, "First you're gonna drop that shitty tone as if I'm gonna ask you for something you can't do." I clenched my jaw as I spoke and could feel my blood pressure going up, "But what you're going to promise me is that you will never, under any circumstances, never interfere with my life again."

Greg stared stoically, his arms on the arm rests of the chair as he drummed the fingers of both hands, slightly shaking his head, "I hadn't planned on it."

"Then it won't be a hard promise to keep."

He shook his head, "No."

I stood up, taking a last look around and decided to hit him with one parting jab, "I know people like you think because I don't scream hurtful shit and make a scene that means I'm weak. I assure you, I'm not weak. I just don't feel the need to make an ugly scene to prove what an asshole you are. You already know."

He let out a heavy sigh, "Are you gonna tell Charlie?"

I threw my tote over my shoulder and forced a fake laugh, "Ha - no. It would be the right thing to do for *you* to tell him but it makes absolutely no difference to me."

Greg leaned forward and stuffed his face in his hands as I walked away.

Lynn was already at the office when I arrived. The scent of coffee and cinnamon hung in the air as I put my things down at my desk and joined her in the kitchen.

"How was Costa Rica?" She asked the minute she saw me walking to the coffee pot. She ripped a piece of sticky cinnamon roll and carefully put it in her mouth so as not to smudge her lipstick.

"Fine. Actually, I was really surprised how many American franchises there are down there. I ordered Pizza Hut in San Salvador."

"San Salvador as in El Salvador?" She took a sip of the piping hot coffee from her *Is it Friday yet?* mug.

I couldn't believe I'd made such a mental error.

"Yeah. Hey listen, thank you for the Cinnabon stuff. I'm gonna run and start catching up on emails," I hurried away from the small kitchen table as quickly as possible.

"Wait – " she said before I could clear the door, "how did you guys end up in El Salvador?"

"It's a really short flight," I answered, not turning around until the growing silence forced me to show my face to her.

"Hey, do you wanna organize an office lunch? Like a welcome back to work thing like on Wednesday, we could – "

"Don't even try it." She wiped icing from her fingers on the napkin she held in the same hand as her coffee mug, "What happened?"

"Nothing. Costa Rica for a couple days, El Salvador a couple days both were really nice, I'd go back – "

"Bianca, I don't want to treat you like one of my children but I know when you're avoiding me. Tell me what happened." She took another sip of coffee, "Why did you guys go to El Salvador? You were supposed to be in Costa Rica."

"Have you ever been to El Salvador? It's lovely."

"So, I guess you don't want to tell me?" She waited for me to answer.

It wasn't that I wasn't going to tell her everything but I knew it was way too much to get into at the office. I'd been home for a week and not allowed myself to think about it beyond what Ian said and how much I enjoyed meeting him. I didn't want to insult Lynn. She was a good friend and knew me better than any of my other friends in D.C. And she knew me well enough to know something was wrong. There was just no way for her to know how wrong.

"I had a good time. Isn't that enough for now?" I said taking a seat at my desk and booting up my computer.

"I just wish you'd talk to me. I care."

"I know. And I will. Promise, I will. I just can't right now."

I tried to smile and it seemed like in that moment she understood something because she smiled a warm smile and said, "I'm glad you had a good time. And yeah, an office lunch sounds like a good idea, pick a place and I'll send out an email."

"Thanks."

I sat staring at my computer screen for several minutes trying hard to look busy. The thoughts swirling around my mind didn't let me focus on anything. I tried to write an email to Greg but quickly deleted it. I attempted several times to write an email to Charlie, to no avail. I even had the urge several times throughout the day and especially at lunch time to talk to Lynn. But I couldn't bring myself to join her for lunch that day. I couldn't risk breaking down and telling her everything. I'd already done that with Elle when she got home Sunday night and after crying to her for an hour, I knew I was going to have to try to keep it together.

The conversation would have to wait.

Instead, at lunch time, I sat in my car across the street from the office and smoked a cigarette. I sipped diet Coke from my oversized McDonald's cup and stared into the cold grayness of the afternoon. I couldn't figure out what had gone so wrong – again.

* * *

I didn't know why things seemed to click with Charlie like they did but it was real and he felt it, too. It was clear to me, even that night in the parking lot, I felt it. Greg's intervention made it impossible to know what could have happened between us. His interference reminded me of other relationships I'd lost because someone interfered. I knew all-too-well there's no such thing as "well-meaning manipulation".

What hurt the most was that for once in my life I thought I could have a relationship with someone that had no intention of hurting me. Even if that was just an unfortunate inevitability, just once it wouldn't be their actual intention. It wasn't like I was looking for a husband. I just wanted, just once, for someone to really choose me and put my feelings first. Maybe that's what love really is? I'd felt it for others but never known it for myself. I couldn't recall a time, a day or even a single moment in its smallest measurement that I felt like I was important to a man. Perhaps the unfortunate by-product of never having known the love of a father or maybe just my bad judgment. Whatever the case, I was sure I'd never been loved by any man.

Except maybe one.

I got back to my desk and noticed my voice mail message light was blinking. My heart jumped. Was it Charlie calling to say he'd heard the whole story from Greg and wanted to apologize? At the very least, could it be Greg calling to let me know that he'd come clean to Charlie? I nervously punched in the password to my voice mail and waited for the message to play.

It was one of the site-assigned engineers needing something. I took a deep breath and jotted down the note of what he needed from me. For the rest of the day, every time my phone rang, I thought it'd be Greg. And for every call that wasn't him, I sank deeper into despair. I frantically checked email each time the icon popped up on my desktop and was disappointed each time.

As the afternoon dragged on, I found myself closer and closer to the verge of tears. I went to the ladies' room several times and tried to keep my emotions under control. "Don't you dare cry," I grunted to my reflection in the mirror. "You're fine. You'll be fine." I tried a different tact, "You've been through worse." I mentally scolded myself for being weak and pounded my fists on the vanity. On one of my visits, a woman from a different office on our floor walked in with a cautious smile. I'd seen her before but I didn't know her. I pretended to be checking my contact lenses to try to hide the tears that had begun welling up in my eyes and as she entered a stall, I quickly made my getaway.

Just as I flung the door open of our office suite, Tommy was walking out.

"I was just looking for you to let you know I was leaving."

"OK," I quickly looked down and tried to hide my face.

"What's wrong?" Tommy asked stepping aside so I could enter the office.

"Oh, I had something in one of my contact lenses. I really need to get some new saline or something." I blinked several times and fussed with my eyes.

"I'll be back on Friday. I've gotta run up to Boston for a few days."

"Alright, see you then," I continued the short walk to my desk.

"Wait – I forgot to ask, how was Costa Rica?"

This time I couldn't do it. I couldn't say everything was fine. I couldn't politely smile and say, "I had a good time." I felt my eyes get hot and my throat went dry. I took a deep breath and tried to compose myself. I stood at my desk, my head hung low as I bit my trembling lip and tried to control the overwhelming hurt.

"Well, I went to Costa Rica, the guy I went with told me he completely ruined my chances with another guy because he's a manipulative, jealous asshole so I flipped out and took a commuter flight to El Salvador, where I spilled my guts out to a complete stranger from Holland."

I heard Lynn gasp as she told whomever she was talking to on the phone that she would have to call them back. Tommy immediately walked back into the office, as Lynn joined him at my desk.

"I really can't talk about this," I told them both as they each took turns firing questions about the particulars of my spontaneous utterance.

As tears streamed down my face, I asked them if they would mind not talking about it anymore. Tommy sweetly hugged my neck and patted my head.

"I've got a flight to catch but I'll call you."

Lynn paced in front of my desk, waiting for her turn to talk to me alone. As she watched him leave, she seized her chance, "I knew something fucked up must have happened." She slapped the top of my desk. "I can't even believe this. I mean, I should have known – "

I dabbed my wet face with tissue, "I shouldn't have said anything. I'm sorry."

"I can't believe Schicker did this," she raised her voice, "Ty is gonna – "

"Don't you dare," I growled at her. "You have to promise me you won't say anything."

"Bianca, these are people are supposed to be our friends – "

"No one, Lynn. I'm serious. I'm embarrassed enough."

"Why are you embarrassed? Greg's the one that should be embarrassed. You could've been killed. What if something happened to you in some third world country? You there by yourself, no one even knew where you were."

"Greg knew," I blurted out before I could stop myself.

"Yeah, a lotta fucking good that would have done." She shook her head, "This is so many shades of wrong, girl. I just don't even know where to start." She started pacing again, "Geezus, I don't even wanna think about if something had happened to you."

"I'm fine. Nothing bad happened." I hung my head, "Anyway, serves me right for picking up a guy in a bar and trying to fuck him within a few hours of meeting him."

"Wait, you think you deserved this? You should be pissed at what Schicker did to you – at what they both did to you."

"I don't wanna fight about how I should feel," I fought back the tears that were once again threatening. "I really need to get back to work. Bill left a message that he needs – "

"This isn't right."

"Please, Lynn," I pleaded with her. Just then my phone rang, "See, I have to get back to it," I didn't even look at the caller ID as I picked up the phone. "Hi, it's Bianca."

"Hi."

I recognized the voice immediately and hung up the phone.

Lynn was on her way back to her desk but stopped as soon as I hung up, "Who was it?"

"No one."

"They hung up?" She stood half-way between my desk and hers, a quizzical look on her face.

"Um-hm." I uttered, dazed just as the phone rang again. This time I didn't reach for it. Lynn immediately knew what was happening. She charged over to my desk and grabbed the phone. "Don't," I said as she picked up the receiver.

"She doesn't have anything to say to you." She then moved the phone from her ear and handed it to me with a whisper, "It's Charlie."

I took the phone from her and hung it up, "I know," I exhaled. "Hey, I gotta get this stuff for Bill, he's waiting," I turned my back to her so I could start looking for anything that would look like it needed immediate attention. I pulled out an old fax and read it as though it was a crucial document.

Lynn squeezed my shoulder and agreed to let me get back to work, "Don't blame yourself for other people's shit. You're too good for that."

I tried to look busy but couldn't help wondering why Charlie was calling. I'd been hoping for that call all day, for months actually. Yet when I heard his voice, I couldn't even allow myself to listen. Fight or flight. I always chose "flight". Maybe Jeff was right. I feel even the slightest emotional pain so strongly that any pain, intentional or not, is unbearable. I looked at the long vertical scar on my left wrist that was now hardly visible. I ran my right index finger over the once very painful wound, "Time heals all," I thought to myself and got back to work.

"This doesn't make any sense. You have to stop."

"Why? What's wrong?" I tried to keep his hands from wriggling free from mine.

"Just stop. You don't really wanna do this," he protested and finally broke free. I knew he had the strength but was being careful not to hurt me in the process of gaining his freedom.

"I do. I really do. You know how I feel about you, Tom," I tried to wrap my arms around his neck but his hands flailed and fought to keep from my embrace.

"You're upset. I understand. But this isn't right. It's not supposed to be like this," he took a step away from me and started to turn his back to me then seemed to second guess the decision.

"I thought we had a connection. I thought you wanted me," I ran my fingers through my hair, confused and somewhat embarrassed. "I thought if I just insisted, you'd eventually give in."

"Is that what you want? You want to wear me down?"

"No. I mean, I thought you were being respectful and – "

"I am," he interjected, his tone softened and he finally did turn his back on me. "Why can't you just take no for my answer? Why do you have to continue to push?"

And there it was.

"I don't know," I said as I slid down into the hardwood kitchen chair, "I really don't know."

"Do you think that's what part of the problem is? I mean, not just with me but with Charlie, too?"

An unfamiliar anger rose up inside of me and I pounded my fist on the table, "Get the fuck out of my house!" My shouting startled Lucy and sent her scampering down the hall to the master bedroom.

"Let me explain."

"Get the fuck out!" I was seething with skyrocketing vehemence.

"Just listen to me, Bianca," he kept his composure as mine went out the window.

"How dare you?" I stayed glued to my chair, at least for the moment.

"Just hear me out."

"You need to leave before I say something we'll both regret."

"I'm trying to help you."

"No, you're trying to embarrass me and I've had enough of that," I stood up and started to try to push him toward the front door. Now it was his turn to hold onto me.

He grabbed my arms as I pushed him, "You think for one second I wouldn't make love to you if I could?"

I tried to pull myself free but he held me a little tighter, "You think it's easy turning down the opportunity to make love to a beautiful woman like you?"

"A slut like me," I glared at him.

"Who said slut? Why are you trying to make this something it's not? I'm your friend. I care about you. I don't need to be another man that's gonna disappoint you. And I would, Bianca."

"Sorry. I mistook your kindness. Forgive me," my sarcastic tone even surprised me.

He shook his head, "I'm saying, think about it. Why is this so hard for you to understand? A guy like me, a man who has children your age, your boss even."

"Here we go. OK, fire me."

"See, that's what I mean." He tugged on both of my hands for emphasis, "Can't you just take this for what it is? If I thought for one minute – "

"Just go," I was trying to keep the lump in my throat from choking me.

"You are a beautiful, amazing woman and if things were different, you would have been in my bed months ago. But it can't happen. Don't you understand that? It's not you, it's not me, it's the situation."

I'd heard this speech once before but that ended much differently than this ever could. Nothing and no one would ever compare to what I'd gone through with Jeff Syddall and now standing here with my good friend begging me to understand why he didn't want to sleep with me, I could feel my hands relax in his as I surrendered. He was right and I knew it.

He let go of my hands, "I'm not trying to hurt you."

"I know," I returned to the kitchen and stood by the table expecting him to leave.

He didn't.

Instead he came into the kitchen, standing in front of me. I averted my eyes but he kept tilting his head and bending at the knees so he could get my attention. I finally looked at him. His tie was still loose from where I'd tugged on it several minutes earlier, his shirt was partially untucked but he looked as composed as ever. He shoved his hands deep into his pants pockets and smiled, "Can we have that coffee now?"

That's how I'd gotten him to my house. I said I wanted to talk over some coffee.

"I didn't make any," I laughed and cried all at the same time, tears rolling down my cheeks as I squeezed my eyes closed in embarrassment.

"Well, let's make some." Having been to my house for coffee several times, he'd apparently paid attention to where things were kept and moved swiftly through the task of putting on a pot of coffee as I just stood there wondering how I'd ever live down the shame I was experiencing at that moment.

As the smell of brewing coffee wafted through the kitchen, Tommy removed two coffee mugs from the built-in rack under the center cabinet above the sink and brought them to the table.

"Sit down," he said putting the mugs on opposite sides of the table, "I'll take care of this."

"I just don't know what to say," I remained standing and wondered if I'd ever be able to look at him again.

"Come on," he put his hand on my back and escorted me to the chair I'd previously been sitting on, "sit here and relax a minute." He spun around to the fridge, opened it and peered in, "You take yours extra light, extra sweet, right?"

He remembered that also.

Tommy sat quietly sipping his coffee waiting for me to begin. Several times I wanted to speak but couldn't. What was there to say? I had no idea why I was pursuing something I knew wasn't right. There was no way I could really see myself with Dr. Thomas Payton. Besides all the reasons he mentioned, I knew we weren't a match. He was so down-to-earth and humble that I sometimes forgot he was a renowned scientist and almost twice my age. He moved effortlessly through the world and his confidence was very attractive to me, even now, making me coffee in my own home. Who does that? Maybe he was the closest thing to a father-figure I'd ever had or maybe I just admired him for being so kind to me. Perhaps gratitude turned to something else and I was just too confused to see it.

I felt a pit in my stomach as I mindlessly stirred my coffee, "All I can say is I'm sorry." I stared into my coffee cup.

"I've never seen you like this."

He was right. I'd lied to him, told him I wanted to talk, told him I needed a friend. "Let's talk over some coffee…" was all I had to say and I knew Tom would be there. He had a place in his heart for me for some reason. Maybe I reminded him of someone, perhaps one of his daughters or all of them. Maybe he hoped if they ever needed someone, there would be someone like him there for them since he couldn't be.

Tommy Payton's wife of 12 years divorced him and took their three daughters back to Monterey, California where they'd met. She was an aspiring ballroom dancer, he was a brilliant nuclear physicist finishing his doctoral thesis. Within a few years, they were married with two daughters and one on the way. When Tommy's career took them to Washington D.C., the marriage began to fall apart. Despite his devotion to her and the children, she grew unsatisfied and eventually began an affair with her ballroom dance partner. Mrs. Payton, whose first name I still don't know, was a striking blonde woman. There was a photo on the credenza in Tom's office of them together after a dance competition. Her heavy makeup drew attention to the deep wrinkles and sun damage visible around her eyes and forehead. In the photo, Tommy gleamed with pride while her smile looked forced and uncomfortable. He once told me it was the last photo they'd taken together. It remained a permanent part of the photo gallery in his office even though his ex-wife had been remarried for years.

Although he doted on his girls, he said they were happier in Northern California with their mother's wealthy parents and step-father's B-list celebrity friends, courtesy of his technical advice on some film about ballroom dancing. And while even his personalized license plates reflected his affection for them, as long as I'd known him, he never said anything about his daughters coming to visit him.

Sitting here now, listening to Elle's favorite Elton John album, I felt ashamed. I didn't even like Elton John but I knew Tommy did. It was just like the bottle of Chenin Blanc I had chilling in the fridge. I didn't even drink wine but I knew that was Tommy's favorite. And just as Sir

Elton whined his way through the song "Tiny Dancer" I had to get up and turn the sound system off.

"Where you going?" He asked surprised by my sudden move.

"I fucking hate this song," I said stalking to the component rack in the adjacent room.

Tom let out a laugh and snapped his fingers, "I should've known something was up as soon as I heard Elton John."

I stopped and smiled at him, I could see him wink and smile back. As I came back into the kitchen, I tied my belted cardigan sweater and tried to cover up what I'd purposely had on display earlier. I was wearing grey sweat pants and a white sleeveless t-shirt, a sheer beige bra that was visible through the fabric showed my once erect nipples. The belted, dark blue cardigan had remained open until just this moment, when I decided to let Tom Payton be my friend.

"I feel like shit Tommy. I mean, I wanted you. I mean, I still do."

"No you don't and that's alright. Now sitting here thinking about it, you know it would have been a mistake."

"A fun mistake maybe," I said trying to smile.

"So, do you wanna talk about it?"

"Not right now."

"OK well, after I finish this, do you mind if I get going?"

"Probably a good idea."

He didn't rush through his coffee but enjoyed it, occasionally shaking his head and smiling at me. I wanted to ask what he was thinking but it occurred to me that I probably didn't need to know. No matter what the answer, what I had been thinking was out of the question.

He set his mug down gently on the table and I knew he'd finished his beverage. A moment later, we both got up. He walked over to the sink and started to rinse his coffee mug, "Leave that. I'll get it." I waved him toward the doorway of the kitchen where I stood waiting for him so I could walk him out.

He nodded, tucking his shirt into his pants and following me through the living room to the front door. He took his coat off of the banister and gently slipped into it, "Can I give you some advice? Call it insight."

I nodded.

"If a man is rejecting you, it may have more to do with him than you," he squeezed my hand with one of his. I swung the door open and watched him leave. As he got into his car he waved, as was his usual but I could see a certain sadness on his face. I took several deep breaths and tried to relax. Maybe it would be alright? But after only a few minutes I found myself at my laptop composing an email.

I know it's been a while, I hope you made it home safely. I was thinking about everything you said. If the offer still stands, please call me…

It had been over a week since Charlie starting calling. He emailed twice over the weekend and left several messages on my voice mail. He didn't say a lot other than "we need to talk". Although it was exactly what I'd wanted for so long, I suddenly didn't know what to say to him. And rather than say the wrong thing, I decided to say nothing.

Ian emailed me asking if there was a way I could meet him in Mexico City in early February. I wasn't sure how I'd be able to do it until Lynn reminded me I had three personal days as of the beginning of the year. I wasn't going to tell her what I was thinking but more than being the Office Manager, she was my friend and I felt I had to be honest with her.

Ian called with the details and said that since we'd actually be going to visit a customer, it would be considered an interview/training and the company would reimburse me for my expenses. We agreed to meet at the Fiesta Americana the morning of the 8th. I feverishly jotted down notes of who we'd be meeting and their titles. He advised that on this particular visit, we'd be seeing one of his biggest customers so that would mean we'd be taking all of our meals with at least a few but up-to as many as a dozen salesmen at any one time. "So don't make any plans to shop or anything fun." I could hear him take a drag of his cigarette, "I know you can do this. They will love you. And they will be happy to have someone that speaks the language."

"You speak the language," I giggled.

"But I'm not Latino," he said in his distinct Dutch accent.

He emailed the hotel information even before we'd hung up the phone. Elle was in Kansas City on business but I thought I should run everything by her. I left her a voicemail which she immediately returned and while giving a quick glance over her calendar said, "I told you, you don't have to run your plans by me, chic. You do what you have to do. I'll be home Tuesday, tell me all the details. I'm so excited for you."

Although I was going to do it even if there was a schedule conflict with her, I knew she appreciated the consideration.

I got online and found flights, a reasonable fare with a decent schedule to get me in the night before our first meetings and proudly began researching the area we were going to visit. Even though I knew it would be work, I was ecstatic about the chance to make such a huge career jump from admin to international sales.

A few hours later, my cell phone rang. I looked at the caller ID and saw it was Charlie's cell number. I put the phone back down without answering it and continued my quest for information.

Moments later, the doorbell rang. I looked at the clock on the far wall in the kitchen, it was after nine o'clock. Lucy was going crazy in the foyer. I picked her up and flipped on the front porch light. I moved the shears out of the way and looked out the side glass of the front door.

Standing there hanging his head was Charlie.

Instinctively, I wanted to hide. What did he want? Why was he here? How did he find out where I lived? There was only one way to know.

Lucy squirmed in my arms as I opened the door. Charlie pursed his lips, "Hi, Bianca."

I said nothing, leaving the door open and walked away to take Lucy to Elle's bedroom. I heard the front door close as I placed Lucy on the bed and closed the door. Charlie was standing in the foyer and called out as I walked back into the living room, "I called you but you didn't answer. I hope you don't mind, I saw the lights on so I thought I'd take a chance and see if you were home."

He was wearing a long, dark wool coat over his Hugo Boss oxford and perfectly-fitting jeans, "May I come in?"

I didn't invite him in but I didn't tell him to leave either. I walked over to the sofa where I'd been working and organized my notes so I could put them away.

"I'm sorry to drop in like this. I didn't know what else to do," he stuffed his gloves into his coat pockets. "You're only wearing shorts and a t-shirt? It's pretty cold outside."

"I'm inside," I said not making eye contact with him, still organizing my notes into the different colored folders I'd bought to keep myself organized.

"Yeah, I guess that was a stupid thing to say," he sighed. "Nice house. I've never been down this way."

"What do you want?"

"I wanted to talk to you. May I take my coat off?"

As I clicked my laptop closed, I looked up at him. He looked peaceful or was it humble?

"Take everything off," I walked toward him, then passed him to turn off the porch light. I hit the lights for the living room and foyer, too. Suddenly, there was darkness except for the diffused light from the television.

He looked confused as he took off his coat, "Where should I put this?"

I took the coat from his hands and hung it over the banister behind him. I began unbuttoning his shirt as he pulled off his shoes using only his feet, his hands were reluctant to touch me but I could feel his fingers gently touching my arms as he tried to pull me to him for a kiss.

"Bianca, can we talk?"

I didn't answer but covered his mouth with mine while working on his belt. Within a few quick seconds, he was almost completely naked, stepping out of his jeans that lay in a pile on the hardwood floor, he kissed me feverishly, mussing up my hair as he held my head.

He gently pushed me away, "Please, I have to talk to you."

I said nothing and led him up the three steps into the living room, to the sofa.

He moaned when I put my hands into his boxers and began fondling him. I pressed myself into him and made him sit down on the sofa. It was torture for me, my heart racing as I pinned him down with my body, pulling back so I could take his erection out of his boxers. I stroked his stiff, warm cock slowly while gently breathing in his ear, "No talking."

"What are you doing?" He asked breathless, gasping as I continued stroking him, pushing my tongue into his mouth. I pulled back, taking off my t-shirt and pressed my body back into his, my arms now wrapped around his neck, I playfully bit his bottom lip before kissing him again.

We kissed long and slow for several minutes, his hands on my cheeks, he gently pushed my face from his, "Please, tell me you forgive me."

I put my mouth on his neck, sucking his flesh intermittently harder then softer. I grabbed a handful of his hair, pulling his head back and placing my mouth on his. His breath was heavy and I knew by the way he kissed me that he longed to be inside of me, his cock twitching as it pressed against the crotch of my shorts. I could feel the wetness from my arousal, every inch of my skin alive and sensitive.

All at once I climbed off of him. I took my bra off, casually tossing it onto the chair immediately to my right. Charlie's eyes locked with mine, I pushed my shorts down, stepping out of them to reveal a small, well-groomed patch of hair and glistening womanhood. I bent down to pick up my shorts, my face moving directly between Charlie's naked thighs, and tossed them to the same chair with my bra.

I stood there for a moment, looking at this gorgeous man sitting on my sofa, his cock erect and ready, his lips parted in anticipation of my next move, he drew in a deep breath and exhaled slowly. I looked at the front door, then gingerly walking down the steps to the foyer I said to him in a glib tone, "I really am in the middle of a lot of things right now. You should go." I flipped on the lights, rudely flooding the entire area with bright light.

He sounded dazed, "What?"

"You know the way out," I said descending the stairs to the basement.

Once I got downstairs, I ran the shower, put on my robe and waited in the main part of the basement to make sure he left. It took several minutes but he did eventually leave, even being polite enough to turn off the lights.

I looked at my reflection in the bathroom mirror, my hair a mess from his hands and decided it was a good idea to wash the smell of Charlie Diaz off of me.

I couldn't believe what had just happened. She just left me sitting there with a rock hard erection and breathless. I heard the shower start as I gathered my clothes from the foyer floor and got dressed. I sat on the sofa for several minutes before conceding she was serious and really wanted me to leave.

Looking around the room, I noticed the laptop and stack of folders. I wondered what Bianca had been working on before I interrupted her. I glanced over and saw a yellow sticky note on top of the stack of folders.

DCA – DFW – MEX

"Travel arrangements for her boss," I thought to myself. I took one last look around the living room, seeing her clothes still slung over the chair that flanked the sofa but decided it was best for me to leave. I turned off the lights and made sure the door was locked as I left.

Driving home, I couldn't help thinking about everything that had happened. I wasn't sure what I'd expected going to her house but I didn't expect this.

I hadn't expected any of this.

* * *

I remember the first time Ty mentioned Bianca at lunch with Greg and me, "Charlie, you should come by the Westin after work on Friday, there's someone you gotta meet."

Greg was quiet as Ty described her, "She kinda tall, probably 5'6" –"

"Tall compared to Diaz over here," Greg chuckled to himself.

Ty continued, "She's from L.A. – "

"Actually, she's from Chicago," Greg interjected, a certain sound of arrogance rang in his tone.

Ty cleared his throat and once again continued, "She's got a really nice smile."

"So, you know what that means," Greg said sarcastically.

"Schicker, what the hell, man? You telling me she's not pretty?"

Greg gave our friend a blank look and shrugged.

I wasn't sure what problem Greg had with her but it certainly seemed there was something, "So, what makes you think I'd like her?" Finishing my iced tea, I flagged the waitress for more. She sheepishly brought over the pitcher to refill it.

"GQ strikes again."

"Fucking asshole. I told you not to call me that."

"What? It's your curse to live with," Greg raised his glass so the waitress would refill his tea also.

"Anyway," Ty continued, "I'm not sure."

"OK, well I'm not interested in picking up a bar fly."

"She's no more a bar fly than I am," Ty insisted. "She's a nice girl."

"Girl?"

"She's 24 or 25, I think. I dunno, I just know she's younger than me," he laughed.

"Might be a little young for me."

"Whatever, you never hang out anymore. Come shoot some stick. I'll be happy to take your money."

"Isn't gambling illegal? What kinda lawyer are you?" I smiled at Ty. "The D.C. kind," he laughed at himself.

* * *

I don't even remember what Greg said when he introduced us. I could barely remember my own name when I saw her. She was friendly, her brown eyes were soft, her smile warm. She had the most gorgeous mouth, a Cupid's bow on the top lip and a full bottom lip, and the way she tucked her hair behind her ear was absolutely adorable. There was just something about her that made her so intimidating to me. She wasn't "model" pretty, she was *beautiful*. Her shoulder-length brown hair was shiny and straight. Her understated makeup and classic suit were more of a turn-on than any overly made up, mini-skirted woman in the bar.

But it wasn't her looks. It was something about *her*.

As that evening went on, I wanted to talk to her but I didn't know how. I asked Ty if he would invite her to play pool with us when Greg insisted it would be better coming from him.

I was surprised how well we got along and so immediately. It usually took me a while to warm up to a woman, try to figure her out but with Bianca, I was just me. I was a little quiet in the beginning but she made me feel so comfortable, so at ease with myself and her. It was the most comfortable I could ever remember feeling with a woman. I took every opportunity I could to get close to her. I loved the smell of her shampoo or maybe it was body wash, it definitely wasn't perfume. It was subtle, you had to get very close to appreciate it.

I noticed her intrinsic sense of angles and set up, even though she claimed she wasn't any good at pool. She humored me while I gave her advice and explained the game, anything to be near her. After one particularly good shot, she squealed and threw her arms around me in a spontaneous celebratory hug. I held her as long as I could while trying not to show how much I liked her. As the evening went on, I couldn't help it. I was smitten.

I told myself when she left, I'd ask if I could walk her to her car but as she announced she was leaving, I lost my nerve. I watched her exit out the side door of the bar, when Ty nudged me with his elbow, "Go after her, man."

I slapped his arm, "Be right back."

I trotted down the stairs that led from the side door of the bar to the main floor of the lobby, past the bathrooms and a small bank of pay-phones to the mostly deserted hallway that went directly into the side parking lot of the hotel. I didn't want to scare her but I also didn't want to call out. I think she knew I was following her and if she minded the intrusion, certainly she would have turned around and said something.

When we got outside, I'd lost my nerve again. Even with our hugging and playful nudging for hours, once alone with her, I didn't know what I should do. My heart raced as I got close, lightly touching her waist as she leaned against her car. The best I could come up with was to tell her I just wanted to make sure she got home alright. She was sweet to play along but I suspect she knew I was covering for ulterior motives.

We looked in each other's eyes for several minutes, not even paying attention to the chill that nipped the air. I felt warm all over being near her. I asked if I could kiss her, my knees going weak when she replied, "Where?" Her voice was breathy, the smile that crept across her lips told me she knew how sexy she was. And in that moment, I knew this wouldn't be the last time I would be with her.

I was desperate to kiss her mouth but something told me to take my time. Instead, I gently held her neck, my thumb touching her ear as I kissed one cheek, then brushing my lips across hers, kissed the other cheek. We looked deep in each other's eyes for a few seconds, lingering in the tender moment before she moved, gently using her body to push mine away from hers. I didn't realize I had her pinned to the drivers' side door of her car.

I thought we'd only been outside a few minutes but in reality it had probably been some amount of time because when I walked back toward the hotel, I saw Greg in the doorway watching us.

"I was just wondering if you guys left," he said as I swung the door open.

"Just saying good night."

Before Bianca got in her car, she had shoved something in my hand and it was only as I walked back to the bar that I thought to look at it. It was my business card that I'd given her after we'd finished shooting pool. My heart sank for a moment until I turned it over and saw her note:

I had a great time. If you ever need a partner ... Bianca (301) 345.2255

I smiled and smoothed the card in my hand, "She's fucking amazing," I said to myself under the ambient lobby noise.

"What?" Greg asked as we ascended the stairs.

"Nothing," I wanted to keep the moment to myself. I left soon after she did and contemplated the right excuse or opportunity to call her. I remembered Greg saying something about Bianca looking for a new place to live. "I could offer to help a friend find a place to live..."

That was the first night that I dreamt of her. Of *us*.

The next day, I dove head-first into apartment hunting as though I was the one that needed a place to live. I found some great buildings on my side of the Beltway. It was only ten o'clock in the morning and I had already started to dial her number at least a dozen times.

Ty texted me late that morning simply saying, "I told you so" and I knew exactly what he was talking about. He was talking about her, and he was absolutely right. I didn't respond to the message, I simply smiled and put my phone back in my pocket.

I did everything I could think of to avoid calling her. I ran errands, went jogging, even did my own laundry for the first time in years, anything to keep myself from dialing her number. I had a date to play racquetball with Schicker but not until later that afternoon and the day seemed to drag on as if the laws of physics had changed since I met her. Getting to see her again couldn't come quickly enough. I found myself driving toward Rockville even before she'd invited me over. I was suddenly embarrassed and didn't want to admit that I was already in her neighborhood when we made a plan to get together the next day to go apartment hunting. My cell phone died before I could confirm a time with her and moments later when I got pulled over by a Montgomery County cop for driving seven miles over the posted speed limit, I was reminded why I didn't live on this side of the Beltway. Still, I looked forward to seeing Bianca the next day and even thanked the Officer for the ticket. Nothing could wipe the smile from my face.

That night, I tried to stop my mind from wondering what it would be like to make love to her. I didn't want to get ahead of myself or pressure her. The truth was, she was the most naturally beautiful woman I'd ever met. Her "one-of-the-guys" ease was alluring. The way she'd push her bangs from her eyes before lining up a shot was truly sexy. Every time I thought about her, I smiled. I remembered touching her soft hair and became erect. I pressed my eyes shut and tried to shake the thoughts from my head.

As I drove to her apartment Sunday morning, I knew it was early but I couldn't help it. I'd slept as long as I could and didn't want to wait any longer to see her. I picked up coffee and thought I'd be nonchalant and act like it was perfectly normal to arrive at eight o'clock in the morning without so much as a phone call. The truth was, I didn't call her because I couldn't find my cell phone. I hadn't seen it since I played racquetball with Schicker the day before and even though I scoured the locker room and checked with the "lost and found" at the gym before I went to her place that morning, I never found it.

She swung the door open wearing only panties and an oversized t-shirt. I simply couldn't control myself. I walked past her, put the coffee down, pulled her into my arms and began kissing her. I felt like I was going to explode. I wanted to feel her skin on mine, her body still warm from sleep, I pulled my shirt up over my head and kicked off my shoes as we stumbled toward the bed. I could feel her kissing me deeply as I pinned her to the bed. I opened my eyes and watched her kiss me, when she opened her eyes and saw me watching her, she smiled into my mouth and held me tighter. Her ease was the sexiest thing about her. I hummed into her mouth and told her how beautiful she was. She rolled over on top of me and I knew I had to stop before I went too far. I didn't want to move too fast. I wanted to seduce her, so I abruptly ended our makeout session, which seemed to upset her.

I asked her if she was mad but she assured me she wasn't. We sipped coffee for a moment before she excused herself to take a shower so we could start our day.

When she left to take a shower, I drank a glass of water and tried to calm myself. I was embarrassed for accosting her but kissing her was everything I'd imagined. Her mouth was so skilled, her body soft and curvy in all the right places. I had every intention of making love to her and I knew when we did, it would be incredible. Just kissing her was the most genuine passion I'd ever felt.

We spent the morning looking at apartments on my side of the Capital Beltway, places close to where I lived. She remarked about the beautiful neighborhoods and brick buildings but never asked why I had taken her there when she clearly had her own ideas of where she wanted to consider. I struggled to keep from telling her we were in my neighborhood. I wanted to show off my well-appointed carriage-style house that my high-priced D.C. designer had decorated for me but something told me she wouldn't be impressed. She didn't seem to show interest in the bullshit that most of the women I'd met seemed to care about. It was one of the things I liked most about her. I guess maybe she was just a genuine person. Perhaps that's what had impressed me about her since we first met. Genuine wasn't something I found in people often and with Bianca, it was as obvious as her soulful brown eyes.

As we drove from property to property, we talked about the things people living in D.C. talk about – politics and traffic.

"I would get so lost coming out this way. Thank you for bringing me over here," she let her head fall back on the head rest and looked over at me with the most adoring smile, her eyes blinking slowly. If I could, I would have leaned over and kissed her right in that moment but going 70 miles per hour on the highway, it wasn't a good idea.

There were pauses in the conversation but nothing uncomfortable. Actually, it was the opposite. There was nothing forced or strained about our time together. Even in silence she was seductive. She'd look over at me from time-to-time and melt me with a perfect, sincere smile. Not a fake, veneer-perfect smile. She had the kind of smile that she and nature worked on. I was amazed at how she beamed brightly at everyone we met. She found beauty and pointed out an upside to every place we visited. Every place seemed ideal from how she described it.

"It's up four flights of stairs. Imagine coming home from grocery shopping."

"Being on the fourth floor, I'd have less of a chance of getting robbed and since the average fire truck ladder goes up seven stories I'm still safe as far as that goes. And, I don't have to worry about Peeping Tom's." She winked at me and giggled, "Plus, look at the view from the bedroom window." She took my hand and led me to the back of the unit. I kissed her hand as we gazed into the peaceful College Park neighborhood.

"You're right," I kissed her hand again.

The last apartment complex we visited was back on the Montgomery County side of the Beltway. It was a conventional apartment complex complete with a club house, day care and tennis courts. As the leasing agent showed us around the empty unit she asked, "Will it be just the two of you?"

I could feel my pulse begin to race at the mere suggestion. It was the same feeling I'd had back at her apartment. It was all I could do to get the agent to leave us. I asked Bianca if she'd noticed the size of the bathroom and grabbed her hand to take her there. Really, I just wanted to touch her and couldn't help myself. When we got to the bathroom, I could feel myself tensing. I turned her around and held her close, staring at our reflection large, well-lit mirror. We looked like we belonged together. We looked happy. She smiled and leaned into me, resting her head on my shoulder as I caressed her. I knew she could feel my excitement growing and seemed comfortable with my arousal and her own. As much as I wanted to be in her in that moment, I couldn't do it. Not like this. She wasn't just some woman that thought I was handsome. She didn't look at me and see dollar signs. There was no way she could fake the adoration in her eyes. No way could she fake those smiles. No way could she fake the passion in her kiss. I'd only known her one day and I was already addicted to the feeling I got from being with her. I was in my mid-30's and I'd never known a woman like her. There was no way I would treat her like some kind of slut. Making love to her would have to wait.

She wanted to go back to her place but I was starving. It was well into lunch time and being at the club at six o'clock that morning looking for my phone, I hadn't had breakfast. Since I woke her up, I knew she hadn't had breakfast either. So we decided to have lunch at a local brew pub not far from the last apartment.

Conversation flowed freely as before but this time we talked a little bit about ourselves. Of course, I gave her the edited version of my life where everything seemed normal.

Close relationship with my grandmother. Code for – my whore of a mother abandoned me to her mother when I was six years old.

An only child. Code for – who knows where my father is and if he has any kids. And who cares if my mother ever had any more.

143

Avid runner. Code for – I was never good at team sports.

Our biggest obstacle that day didn't come from either of us.

At the end of our meal, when Bianca excused herself to the ladies' room, a woman came over and introduced herself, then invited herself to take Bianca's seat at our table. I was amused by the stranger's advances and didn't even catch her name. I just sat back in my chair and drummed the fingers of my right hand on the table as my left arm was draped over the back of my chair. Everything in my body language had to tell this woman I thought she was a joke. And indeed, she was. Even if I had been attracted to her, the moment she approached me, I knew she had no respect for herself or me. She chatted on about having noticed me when I walked in and asked if I lived in the neighborhood. I didn't answer any of her questions and instead smiled at her as she nervously made her pitch but Bianca got back before the woman could do much more than watch us leave.

I could see my date was upset, she was the kind of person whose face reflected her feelings but she didn't ask about the woman until I prodded her when we got back to her apartment. She admitted her jealousy, a chance for me to reassure her that she had nothing to worry about, "I'm exactly where I want to be." I needed her to know it and believe it because I'd never meant it more in my life.

Bianca hinted that she wanted me to leave but I did everything I could to extend our time together. She eventually said she really didn't want me to leave so much as she just wanted the opportunity to take a shower. In hind sight, it might have been better if I'd left right then.

After her shower, I asked if I could use the bathroom and made the major faux pas of snooping through her things. I found her body wash and sitting on the edge of the tub, I flipped up the top and drew in a long, deep breath. I squeezed the bottle lightly to release some more of the pleasant lavender scent, not realizing there was a crack toward the bottom. The squeezing caused a large drop of gooey soap onto my jeans near my crotch. I quickly took off my pants and ran the spot under water but the more I rubbed, the more bubbles it made, the bigger the wet spot got. I panicked. I did the only thing I could do to get out of my clothes.

I took a shower.

She seemed surprised but not put off when I left the bathroom wearing only my boxer shorts. I was careful to make sure the wet part of my jeans wouldn't be visible in the neatly folded pile of my clothes that I set on a stool at the breakfast bar.

She pulled a chenille throw over us as we cuddled on the sofa, Bianca's head on my chest, my back nestled in the corner of the sectional sofa watching reruns of Star Trek. I loved being near her but I was also hoping I was giving the denim enough time to dry so I could eventually leave. Although I hadn't entirely talked myself out of sleeping with her that night.

She'd made a few trips to the kitchen over the course of a few hours and eventually mentioned she was hungry. She asked if I wanted to get dressed and get something to eat but I was certain my pants wouldn't be dry enough to go anywhere. When she started talking about what she had in the house, I felt myself panic. She mentioned pizza and quesadillas, neither of which I could eat.

She looked over at me and seemed disappointed by my reluctance. I didn't know how to tell her that my pants were wet so we couldn't go out and being lactose intolerant I couldn't eat what she had on hand. I could feel myself flushed with embarrassment. I decided I'd rather leave than ruin the perfectly wonderful day with a discussion about my faulty digestive system.

I could see by the look on her face she was surprised but I didn't know what else to do. I knew I'd see her again and I'd eventually explain to her what happened. Someday, we would both laugh about it. In that moment, I just needed to get out of there. I got dressed, leaving my shirt untucked from my jeans and made a quick exit. I spent the entire drive home wishing I had my phone so I could at least call her and thank her for such a great day.

"I'll call her tomorrow," I bargained with myself later as I stood in my kitchen eating left over Panda Express.

The next morning as I showered, I thought about the mishap with Bianca's shower gel and laughed out loud, "She must think I'm insane." I continued laughing as I lathered up my hair, wondering what she must have thought when I came out of the bathroom in only my boxer shorts.

As I shaved my face, I thought about the previous afternoon in the model apartment bathroom. I thought back to how good we looked together. Confident and comfortable in each other's arms, our Latino heritage somewhat obvious in our darker hair and facial features although most people mistook me for Italian until they found out my last name.

I sat in Monday morning traffic on my way to work but it didn't bother me as it usually would. It gave me more time to think about Bianca and our day together. "No games," I thought to myself as I crawled along in morning rush.

When I arrived at work, Schicker approached me in the kitchen as I poured my first cup of coffee, "Where were you? We were supposed to watch the game last night."

"I forgot all about that, I'm sorry. I spent the day helping a friend look for a new place to live." I blew on the steaming hot liquid and took a sip, "And I lost my phone."

"So you were with Bianca last night."

"Yeah," I smiled and sipped more coffee. I continued blowing on the top of the full mug, "I should have called you but I kinda had my hands full." I took another careful sip, "It was a really good day though."

Greg walked with me back to my office and sat down on the sofa while I took a seat behind my desk, "Hey, do you know who I have to see about replacing my phone? Is it the IT guys?"

"I have no idea," Greg sounded annoyed, "I've never lost company property. Ask the admin." He put his coffee down on the table next to him and sat back on the sofa, crossing his legs, "You know, she's not exactly a *nice* girl, if you know what I mean."

"No, I don't know what you mean," I took the card with her number on it out of my wallet and put it on the desk in front of me as he continued.

"I mean, she's a good fuck to be sure but I didn't think you'd date her." He smoothed his pant leg, "She's good in bed but not exactly great on paper, if you know what I mean."

I couldn't believe what I was hearing. My jaw hung open as I struggled to try to figure out how to process all the feelings that were passing through me all at one time.

"Hey, it's not *your* fault. I tried to tell her Friday night it wouldn't be cool for her to try to hook up with you but..." his voice tapered off, "I mean, I don't care, do what you want."

"It didn't. I mean, we kissed a little bit but I left, I was home by nine." I felt the need to impress upon my friend that I hadn't slept with the same woman he had, "I really didn't know, Schicker. Had I known, I would have never even called her." I stared at the card on the desk in front of me with her handwriting, "So why the fuck did Ty wanna set us up?"

"Well, he doesn't know anything. No one does. I mean, I didn't say anything to anyone because it wasn't really that big of a deal. She's new in town and I kinda felt bad for her. We were spending a lot of time together and it just kinda happened one night. It's not like I'm dating her or anything."

"Well, like I said, we didn't sleep together."

"There's a surprise." Greg picked up his coffee and took a long drink, "It's my experience that she moves pretty fast."

"Well, yeah, she seemed pissed that I wouldn't," I knew it was an unfair characterization but I was genuinely angry with her in that moment.

"So you didn't even get a blow job or anything? What a shame."

"God, no." I shook my head and took the card from my desk and put it in the middle drawer directly in front of me. "I'm glad you said something. I really don't want any problems."

"No problem, man. I mean, if you wanna go out with her, that's cool."

Greg shrugged, "I've known her a while. I met her before she even moved here. She's friends with a friend's sister. I think she had the hots for me from when we first met but I've kinda kept her dangling for a bit. She might have tried to get with you to make me jealous." He shook his head, "I tried to tell you in an indirect way that it probably wasn't a good idea."

"I guess I wasn't paying attention. Shit. I hate this kinda bullshit." I slapped the top of my desk. I couldn't believe what I was hearing. I was not about to get sucked into games with this woman. Not any woman. And certainly not this woman and one of my best friends. Not again. Never again. "Well, that's the end of that then."

"Whatever you wanna do, man. I was just telling you because I'm not entirely sure it's all about you. Like I said, she might have been trying to make me jealous. Or she can just switch gears that fast. I have no idea."

I shook my head, "Not gonna happen." I took a drink of my coffee. My stomach turned and my head pounded, how could this be happening? How could I be in the middle – again.

* * *

Karen was one of millions of D.C. transplants. Her dye job, fire-red hair and fake nails were an immediate turn-off to me but Schicker worshipped her. She was originally from Little Rock, Arkansas and supposedly graduated from Tulane. She'd come to D.C. looking for her "Mrs." and found Greg Schicker. They had a whirlwind romance and when he flew her to Switzerland for the holidays, she thought she'd met the man that would put her in the lifestyle she believed she deserved. Unfortunately, he was a little too slow popping the big question and her sights wandered.

We were at a company cocktail event when she asked my age and astrological sign. I chuckled and gave her my birthdate telling her I didn't believe in the Zodiac. That night she not only found out I was a few months younger than her boyfriend but also his boss, and began openly flirting with me. Greg said the fawning and constant compliments were part of her charm but it felt a lot like ardor to me. I tried in delicate ways to let her know I wasn't interested in her and not just because she was dating my best friend.

The real trouble came when she insinuated herself between Greg and I under the guise of planning a surprise party for his birthday. She said as his best friend I had to help her but it soon seemed to me this was just a way for her to get my home address and drop by my place any time she wanted. When she openly propositioned me, I immediately rebuffed her and began avoiding her at all costs. I should have told my friend about the encounter but I didn't. I couldn't. I didn't want to be the one to hurt him. I was a coward. When Karen decided to leave Greg for some big shot at NIST, she made sure to tell him she cheated on him with two other men and had tried to seduce me. To this day, I think that was her way of getting back at me for not fucking her. As though breaking Schicker's heart wasn't enough, she had to try to destroy our friendship. It took months before he could look at me and even longer before I could look at him. After what happened with Karen, I vowed I would never let a woman come between us again.

Greg finally left, taking his empty coffee mug and apologizing for the "bad news".

"I can't believe Bianca did this to me," I seethed as I tried to concentrate on anything other than her.

As if I wasn't annoyed enough, the admin told me it'd be a week before I got my new cell phone and my boss was going to have to sign off on the requisition. I was already disenchanted with my boss and top management as a whole but having to get his signature meant I'd have to hear him opine about responsibility or some other such bullshit that I knew full-well was for the benefit of his own ears not mine.

He didn't disappoint. I came away with the paperwork I needed to get my new phone but I was still wracking my brain trying to imagine what I could have done with the one I'd lost. It just wasn't like me to be careless with something like that. I made a deal with myself right then and there that if I ever lost my phone again, I'd sooner resign than have to hear that speech from my boss again.

On Thursday, Greg asked if I was going to the bar, "Yeah, probably. Ty and those guys are trying to test my intestinal fortitude and lack of understanding of basic geometric principles." I gave a half-laugh as he stood in my doorway.

"Alright, well, I was just wondering if you were gonna talk to Bianca or what," he ran his fingers though this hair with one hand and held the door frame with the other.

"No, I'm out of it," I said clapping my hands together once. "You know her better, you tell her. Tell her I don't want any bullshit and ask her to please stop calling me. It's fucking annoying."

151

But as the calls persisted, I asked my friend for some insight. "Why the fuck is she still calling me?" My voice echoed around the racquet-ball court, shoes squeaking as I smashed the small blue ball with every ounce of aggravation I felt.

Breathless, Greg tried to explain, "She just doesn't like to take no for an answer, I guess. I dunno, maybe she wants to hear it from you."

"Not gonna happen," I said missing a point and slamming into the wall, "And what's with how she's always looking at me? I mean, did you explain to her?"

Greg said he explained as best as he could but that she was the kind of girl that had a problem with rejection. He said he'd learned a bit more about her from his friend's wife and that she might just be that crazy girl that boils your pet bunny if she doesn't get her way. It wasn't the Bianca I knew but I knew very little about her and really only from one day. If even her own friends were saying these things, I had to believe it. It did nag at me though because for as often as she called and hung up, and texted things like "pls call me", she only approached me one time. Although I did see her going out of her way to watch me shooting pool or throwing darts, Greg insisted she was looking at him. It didn't matter. There was no way I was going to date her and certainly not after seeing the persistent, almost obsessive, behavior.

"Hey, GQ, I completely understand why women want you. Hell, I'd fuck ya." Greg playfully punched me in the gut as we left the court, our time having been signaled as expired by the flickering of the lights.

I really hated when he called me "GQ" – reference to *Gentleman's Quarterly* magazine. His tone was mocking but not necessarily in a friendly way, it was more like he was insulting me disguised as friendly ribbing. The strange thing was Greg was just as concerned with his looks as I was. He and Ty were both as well-dressed, if not better dressed, than me. I went strictly with designers, they actually had style. Of the three of us, I was probably the least comfortable in my skin. Maybe that was the joke.

I figured if I dressed a certain way, drove a certain car, earned a certain amount of money, I could be just as good – maybe better than my peers. Better because I didn't have the advantage of a mother and father that loved me. Better because in spite of my mother's lies and father's absence I made something of myself. I told myself if I busted ass and graduated Suma, I could be better. If I lived in the right zip code and had the right clothes, I wouldn't have to think about what I didn't have growing up. The better the quality of things in my life, the better quality of my life. And it worked for a while. When my Grandmother was alive, when I could hear the pride in her voice, when she'd look at me lovingly and tell me how proud she was of me, it felt like it had been worth it. I remember her frail hands on top of my head, as she would pray for "travelling saints" to be with me to and from college.

When she was gone, so was the only family I had.

Bianca was the first person I'd met since living in D.C. that I thought could understand me. I thought she could handle all the truth of my life and maybe even help me be a better person for it. The ease between us invited me to tell her everything but I never got the chance. And now it was making sense. She was so comfortable, so effortless because she didn't have anything to lose. She wanted Greg. He was her ultimate goal. The more I thought about it, the angrier I got. I had to do what I could to keep her out of my mind but thoughts of her were never far away. Unfortunately, most of the thoughts were the good ones and all the things I missed about her.

One night, Greg called late and wanted to know if I wanted to go to a card party at Elizabeth's down in the Village. I didn't know her well but she had been especially nice in the past weeks and seemed to be supportive of my decision not to date Bianca. I agreed to go with him although the late hour of two o'clock in the morning seemed strange.

Schicker assured me that Bianca wouldn't be there but as soon as we walked in, there she was. I noticed she had a shot in one hand, a beer in the other. Apparently, she was chasing a buzz.

I found my way upstairs to a bedroom and sat alone wishing I'd never agreed to ride over with Greg. I saw Bianca standing outside the door, contemplating talking to me. I'd hoped she'd resist the temptation to continue the game she was playing with me but she didn't. Instead, she slinked into the room and closed the door. I couldn't even look at her. I wanted to tell her I knew all about Greg but when I did finally look at her, the words left me. All I could manage was a forceful, "Leave me alone."

I felt bad when she broke down crying but figured that's what too much alcohol does to some people. Then I told her she looked like a slut, just to hurt her more. I knew my harsh words would make her cry. I hated myself for doing it, but it was almost as if I couldn't stop myself from lashing out at her.

I'd seen her earlier in the kitchen and told Greg I was going to confront her but he said with Bianca drinking to excess it might end in an ugly scene. As I lumbered down the stairs of Elizabeth's townhouse, I could feel the disapproving looks from the people waiting in line for the bathroom who'd surely overheard my painful words.

Some ugly scenes can't be avoided.

"Can we just go?" I pleaded with Greg on the front stoop of the house.

"I just wanna smoke this Cuban and then we can get outta here," Greg grunted as he held the cigar in his teeth and lit the end. "Get in on one of these, Charlie," he handed me a fresh cigar and a cutter, "Cohibas." He smiled, created a large puff of smoke then proudly blew it in the air.

As I lit up the cigar, I saw Bianca briskly walking to her car.

"Where's Bianca going?" Ty asked, looking at me.

I shrugged my shoulders, "I don't know. She confronted me upstairs and – "

"What happened?" Greg immediately stopped sucking on the cigar and stared at me.

"She asked me what was wrong – "

"What did you say?" His eyes were wide.

"I told her to forget about it, that I had and that she should just move on."

Just then, Elizabeth came out and pushed me off the landing. I was able to keep myself from falling but stumbled down the slight incline, catching myself with my hands.

"What the hell?" I asked her, brushing the dirt from my hands onto my jeans.

"You insulted one of my guests and it's time for you to go."

"Wait – what did you say?" Greg's 6'4" frame suddenly seemed menacing.

"He called her a slut," Elizabeth yelled and once again pushed me off the landing. "You need to leave." She turned and slapped Ty's arm with the back of her hand, "Ty, get this fucker off my property."

"Calm down. Charlie called who a slut?" Ty asked trying to catch up.

"Bianca," Elizabeth answered glaring at me.

I now stood several steps away on the sidewalk, "I didn't call her a slut, I said – "

"Everyone heard what you said. Now, I'm sorry but you need to go."

Ty interjected, "Elizabeth, calm down. He's leaving. Right, Charlie?"

Greg asked Ty to try to calm Elizabeth down and told her we were leaving, then walked over to me looking for the details of what happened.

"Can we just go now?" I had my back to the small crowd that was now gathered at the front door. I was sure my face was as red as my shirt.

"Hey, I didn't know you guys had a fight," he slapped my shoulder and we proceeded to the car. I could hear Elizabeth asking someone to find Bianca but didn't have a chance to hear if anyone told her she'd already left.

I don't know if it was the hour or the smelly cigar but I had a pounding headache by the time I got home.

"Hey, don't worry about all this. It'll blow over," Greg said rather glib as I closed the car door.

He was wrong.

The following week, I took Monday and Tuesday off work. I didn't want to be at the office, I didn't want to be at home. I wanted to call her but then I didn't want to call her. I was confused and irritated. Why was this happening?

"That's not the half of it," Greg said as the waitress put our lunches in front of us that Friday.

"I don't wanna hear it," I cut my sandwich in half and tried to eat.

"She told me you hit her."

"What?" I had to put my food down and take a drink of water, "I didn't fucking touch her." My volume and language were completely inappropriate for where we were.

Greg hushed me and continued, "That's just what she said, I know you wouldn't do that." He picked at his food and continued, "I'm not trying to get in the middle – "

"I know," I interrupted, "I just don't understand what the fuck is going on. She keeps calling me, leaving hang up messages on my voice mail at work. I'm not an idiot. I know it's her. She doesn't hang up until she hears the whole message so it registers the call back number," I wiped my hands on my napkin. Suddenly, my appetite was gone, "And she calls at weird hours." I sighed and took another drink of water, "Why don't you just tell her to stop calling me? For your sake, if not for mine."

He shrugged his shoulders.

"And maybe tell her to quit the fucking lying," I was fuming just thinking about it.

He spoke softly, taking a bite of his burger, "You know what, Charlie? Your best bet is to start seeing someone else."

"Why can't you just – "

He interrupted, "I can and I will but that would probably help some things, too. You know what I mean?"

"Whatever. She's your friend and you're supposed to be my friend. Help me out."

"I'll talk to her."

"Yeah talk to her before they pull my fucking clearance for domestic violence or some bullshit," I put my napkin back on my lap and attempted to eat.

"Look, I know a really nice woman. A lawyer, she's a got a rock hard body. You've met her. Candace. She's great, educated, really good job."

"If she's so great, why don't you date her?"

He shook his head, "I got stuck in the friend zone on this one. But if I could, trust me, I would. But I know for a fact she likes you and she'd take your mind off this shit with Bianca."

"Whatever. Give her my number."

* * *

I spent the next couple weeks trading emails and phone calls with Candace Sullivan, Esquire. She graduated from Baylor and worked at a firm near L'Enfant Plaza. I had no idea what kind of law she practiced and I didn't care enough to ask.

Greg was right about one thing, she did have a rock hard body but her soul seemed to match. There was something so cold about her. She bragged that she worked out three hours a day.

Greg told me every day after our first date how lucky I was and how she was perfect for me. "She likes you a lot Diaz," he stood in the doorway of my office just after lunch, "you gonna call her again?"

"I don't know," I opened my email and searched for anything to get involved in that would extricate me from the conversation.

"You should. She's fantastic and she's really into you," he casually knocked twice on my door and left.

Half-hour later, Candace called and asked me to dinner on Friday night. She insisted on sushi. I hate sushi but respectfully agreed. I had no idea the sushi wouldn't be the most unpleasant thing about the evening.

During dinner, she got a phone call from a friend. To my surprise, I heard her making plans to meet her friend for drinks.

"Oh, I hope you don't mind. A girlfriend of mine is in town and she wanted to meet up tonight."

"Sure," I picked at the sashimi on my plate. "Whenever you need to go is fine with me."

"No, silly. I told her about you, she's dying to meet you."

"OK," I said slightly shaking my head.

"Great. I can't wait for you to meet her. Her name is Sue. You're gonna love her."

It took everything in me not to say, *"Doubtful."* Instead, I asked where we were supposed to meet.

"The Westin."

My head snapped back, "Which Westin?"

"The one by your office."

"Why?" I asked, trying to hide my disapproval.

"That's where she's staying."

"OK," before I could ask, she continued.

"I asked Greg where she should stay and he suggested the Westin. You guys go there a lot, don't you?"

"Well, I've never stayed there but I've gone to the bar now and then for drinks after work."

"Anyway, I told her we'd call her when we got there."

"That's fine," I didn't care one way or another. I had no intention of making this night last any longer than social convention would dictate.

We met Sue just before ten o'clock. Her tight black skirt and even tighter pink, low-cut shirt were a juxtaposition of Candace's conservative attire. She seemed nice enough but what you might call an "airhead". Maybe she was intelligent just not very well-spoken. Like Candace, she had bleach blonde hair and had a slight Southern twang. She said she was in town for work and was sorry to be interfering with our date.

"It's not a problem, really. Actually, I should probably get out of your way and let you ladies – "

"No way, handsome. You're mine tonight," Candace squeezed me uncomfortably hard and rubbed her face on my shoulder.

"Yeah, don't go. Besides, how would it look? Two women alone in a hotel bar?"

I smiled politely and walked with the women through the dense Friday night crowd. I hadn't been to "happy hour" at the Westin since Elizabeth's party as I thought it best to avoid anyone that knew Bianca. Thankfully, it was probably too late for my usual group of friends but the bar was plenty busy. I found a table on the perimeter of the dance floor and led the women, one on each arm, down the stairs to the table.

I stood there as the women drank fuzzy navels, talking about old friends from school and general gossip about people I didn't know. I was surprised at my patience. I didn't want to be with Candace. I certainly didn't want to be there with her and her friend but there was something familiar and pleasant about being there.

"Do you ladies wanna shoot some pool?" I leaned in and asked over the loud Motown music.

"I don't think so," Candace answered as though it was the most ridiculous question she'd ever heard.

I nodded my head and went back to observing other people who seemed like they were not only happy to be there but happy with the company they were keeping. I remembered being happy there once.

I was surprised when the two women suddenly dismissed themselves from the table. I couldn't hear their conversation over the loud music and because I didn't care, I didn't try.

It was almost fifteen minutes later when they strutted back to the table.

"You ladies want another drink?" I asked, finishing the last of my beer.

"Wait for the waitress," Candace put her arm around me and pulled me to her so I could hear.

"I can go up to the bar."

"No need for that," Sue winked at me.

"What's going on here?" It felt like they knew something I didn't.

They both shrugged, smirks painted on their faces.

"Actually, I was asking Candace if it'd be OK for you to touch my boobs."

"What?" I was stunned and let out a nervous laugh.

"They're new," she said proudly pushing them together apparently embarrassing me more than herself. I continued with the nervous laughter and scanned the room for a waitress. Just then, I noticed Bianca and Lynn at the bar. They seemed to be searching for someone.

All of a sudden, Candace kissed me. I could see over her arm that Lynn and Bianca were looking directly at us. Lynn shot me a look just before spinning around on her barstool.

I pulled Candace's arms from around me and tried to excuse myself.

"No, no, no. You can't go right now," she clung to my neck and sloppily kissed my cheek very close to my ear. I cringed at the wetness of her mouth and pried her arms off of me.

"Where are you going?" Sue shouted over the music and pulled on my arm as I tried to pass her.

"I think I just saw a friend up at the bar. I wanna go say hello."

"No!" Candace shouted and pulled me back to the table.

I instinctively pulled away, "What's the problem here?" Now, I knew something was going on.

"You're gonna go talk to *her*," Candace said, a certain amount of condescension in her voice.

"Who?"

"Your little secretary friend," Sue interjected.

I was shocked they knew who Bianca was. I saw the tense look on her face, realizing she'd said too much.

"I gotta go." I started to leave and then reconsidered, "What did you do?" I walked back to the table and waited for an answer.

The two friends looked blankly at each other and then at me. I could see how uncomfortable they were with the question.

"Someone should tell me right now what the hell is going on," I was trying to be as polite as possible.

"Nothing. I was trying to kiss you, I saw you looking at some other woman and I remembered Greg mentioning some secretary that was running some kinda game on you. He said you met her here, I figured that was her."

"Candace, can I drive you home?" I started to walk away from the table, convinced I didn't get the entire story.

"Charlie, don't go," Sue wailed.

"Candace?" I stood there for a brief moment and then began to walk away.

"Call me!" I heard her shout.

I waved my hand and proceeded up the stairs. I never spoke to her again.

* * *

Greg asked me what happened with Candace but I couldn't explain. I didn't want to explain. I was surprised that he set us up in the first place and more surprised by how disappointed he was when it didn't work out.

We were just finishing up lunch at the club when Greg asked me if I wanted to grab a drink after work on Friday. "Where?" I asked skeptically while fumbling through my wallet for an adequate tip for the waiter.

"Where do you think?" He answered finishing his iced tea and placing his napkin on the table.

"I don't think that's a good idea."

"Look, it's a bunch of us from the office. You have to stop letting this thing run your life. I mean, I know the whole thing at Elizabeth's got ugly but you keeping away is making it seem as though you're guilty about something. If you really didn't do anything wrong, what do you feel bad about?"

"At the very least, I was an asshole."

The waiter cleared our plates as we sat in silence.

"OK then. You're our friend and we want you to come hang out."

"So you think I can show my face around there without Elizabeth or Lynn wanting to kill me?"

"Lynn now, too?"

"Well, I would imagine if she told you some bullshit, she's told Lynn, too. And I notice Ty's not coming around much." I shook my head, "I'll try to make it."

"It's been a while. Don't you think it's time we all just move on?" Greg closed the door to his coupe and rolled the window down. "Why not just put the past in the past?"

Although I was parked next to him, I took my time putting my things in the trunk of my car. I kept wondering when it would feel alright again. When would I go back to being the person I was before I met Bianca. When would I ever stop being so angry at her.

I walked in the door of my house just in time to drop the dry cleaning over a chair and reach for the ringing cell phone in my pocket. I didn't even look at the caller ID, I just answered, "Diaz."

I could hear noise in the background but no one speaking. I heard a voice that sounded like Greg's ask, "Who are you calling?" Then silence. I looked at the screen, "Call ended 0:34". Even all these months later, I knew whose phone number it was.

I thought about calling her back and asking why she called and hung up but I figured that was only playing into her game. I gathered up the now pile of plastic and newly dry-cleaned clothes off of the floor and took them to the bedroom, where I flung them on the bed. I carefully removed the plastic from the clothes and replaced the wire hangers with the wooden ones from my closet.

"I think I *am* up for a happy hour."

The next day, Friday, was the first time in weeks that I'd seen Ty. He stopped by my office just before three o'clock.

"Hey, Charlie. How've you been?" He said plopping down onto one of the guest chairs in front of my desk.

"I'm good. You?" I asked turning from my computer to face him.

"Good. Good. Everything's good." Although he was sitting back in the chair, he seemed to be forcing himself to be at ease with me.

"So, what's going on?" I asked looking to the door wondering if I was going to need to close it.

"Well…" he paused long enough to let me know this would probably need to be a closed-door discussion.

I got up and casually closed the door most of the way, "So what's on your mind?" I returned to my seat.

"I think this thing with you and Bianca has gotten outta hand, man."

"I was afraid you were gonna say something like that."

"Look, I understand you didn't want to date her but the thing at the party and then you getting your girlfriend and her friend to jump her in the bathroom at the bar. I mean, that's a bit much no matter – "

"What?" I asked calmly even though inside I was suddenly frantic.

"Lynn told me some chics jumped Bianca in the bathroom at the Westin and I'm just not sure – "

"Wait a minute," I said louder than I intended and flew to the door to close it. I took a seat on the small sofa on the other side of my office. Ty stood up and leaned against my desk, "I did not have *anyone* do *anything* to her."

"Listen, I know. She's young, she's driving you nuts, whatever. I don't wanna get in the middle of this. We're friends and – "

"Hey, I need you to understand something. I have no idea what happened with Bianca and anyone in any bathroom anywhere." I sat back and ran my hands over my face, "Fuck."

"Look, I've known you a long time, man. We're friends. But I think I'm gonna marry Lynn. At least, I'm gonna propose. Lynn is close to Bianca. So you see where – "

"I understand perfectly."

"Can you just try to be civil when she's around?"

"Ty, I don't even – " I looked over at him as he stood there, arms folded.

"Never mind. I appreciate you stopping by," I walked over to him and patted him on the back as he went to the door. "And hey, I really hope you and Lynn will be happy."

"We'll see," he patted my shoulder, "Take care, Diaz."

"You know me," I said smiling. I turned away from the door, went back to my desk and began composing an email.

Bianca, I'm hoping you read this very carefully as I would like to avoid any further misunderstandings.

I sat staring at the screen for several minutes, wondering how to articulate the thoughts swirling in my head. What really happened at the card party, how she'd lied about me hitting her, the confrontation with the women in the bathroom and how I had nothing to do with it, if it happened at all. But each sentence I typed felt wrong and I'd immediately hit backspace and delete what I'd typed. Really what I wanted to know was, *"Did you ever really want me or was this just a game?"*

I left the email up on my screen as I went around to the other side of the desk and took a seat back on the small sofa. I put my feet up on the coffee table and tried to read up on an upcoming project in Costa Rica.

Schicker walked in a while later, "Hey, did Ty come see you?" He asked turning one of the guest chairs around to face the sofa and taking a seat.

"Yeah," I said not looking up.

"Cool," he cleared his throat. "So, what's up?"

"Just looking over this Costa Rica thing."

"Good, good. You think you're gonna go still this year or wait until January?"

I didn't want to tell him that at that moment, I'd crawl under a rock if I could. "I don't know. I haven't gotten that far."

"Well, I know you're not really much on flying so if you don't wanna go, just let me know."

I ran my fingers through my hair and looked at him, "What?"

"If you don't wanna go to Costa Rica, I'll go," he said slowly, as if I didn't understand English.

"Oh, yeah. OK well, I'm kinda busy right now, I'm not really thinking about Costa Rica."

"I thought you said you were reading up on the Costa Rica project?" He clasped his hands behind his head and crossed his legs, "You alright?"

In exasperation, I put the folder down on the sofa cushion next to me, "Not really. I was just thinking about sending an email to Bianca."

He quickly leaned forward, "Did you?"

"No, I was thinking about it." I took my feet off the coffee table, "I was just hoping we could try to get past all the lies and bullshit. Ty told me some more shit just a while ago and I'm honestly just sick of it."

"I'll talk to her, seriously," he said, getting up to close the door. "I don't think it's a good idea for you to go near this thing."

"Well, if you'd have taken care of this when I first asked you, I wouldn't be dealing with this."

"Don't be so sure," he said returning to his seat.

"Why?"

"Have you heard the name Jeff Syddall?" He asked in almost a whisper, despite the door being closed.

"Should I?" I moved the folder to the coffee table and moved into the corner of the sofa to better face him.

"I know it's probably strange to hear, because I really like Bianca. I've started seeing her in a different light and – "

"Whatever, who's Jeff Syddall?" I interrupted not wanting to hear about his new found affection for a woman he previously referred to as "only a piece of ass".

"Well, I'm not going to pretend to understand why she does the things she does but I think underneath it all she does have a good heart. But I think she is capable of really shitty things."

I sighed and waited for him to continue.

"Jeff Syddall was a high school teacher of hers. She got him fired." He looked down at his hands then looked back at me, "I think you may remind her of him."

"What the fuck are you talking about?" I could feel my heart pounding in my chest, "What the fuck does some teacher gotta do with me?"

"I just know that I've heard her say you remind her of him. And I know this whole thing with the teacher was some kinda ugly business. He's why she moved to L.A."

"I thought she moved to L.A. for her job?"

"Maybe that too but I know the whole situation with the teacher was a factor. And she told me herself that you remind her of Mr. Syddall."

"Mr. Syddall?"

"Her English teacher."

"How did she get him fired? Never mind. I don't care." I waved my hands in front of me then got up and walked back to my desk. I deleted the email I'd been trying to draft to her. "Are you telling me she's gonna try to get me fired?"

"I don't know. I hope not. But that's why I'm gonna run some interference and try to figure out what her deal is."

"Like I said, I don't care what her deal is, I just want to be left alone."

"Totally. I know what you mean, I just wanted to let you know, I've got your back."

My office phone rang and I had to take the call. Just before Schicker left I covered the phone with one hand, "I don't think I'll go with you guys tonight. Alright?"

"No way. You're coming and we're going to stop running from this thing. We're gonna work this out," he winked and left, leaving the door open on his way out.

Toward the end of the day Ty dropped by, "You're gonna be there tonight, right?" He hung on the door and smiled a huge, proud smile.

"I'll be there," I said, not at all expecting that night would change my life as much as it was going to change his.

When I got to the Westin, I saw her sitting there. She looked amazing. Her toned legs peeked out from a slightly flared skirt as she sat on a chair that had been moved to the front of our usual u-shaped booth. The black patent leather pumps she wore added a sexiness to her otherwise modest outfit.

"Schicker's already down there," someone said, although I didn't know who.

I noticed she'd sat up a little straighter when she realized I was there. I stood behind her waiting for Ty and the others to join me, although I was in no hurry to move. It was as though I could feel electricity between us even though we didn't speak a word or even face each other. Call it what you want, there was something between us.

"What are you thinking?" I thought to myself as I trotted down the stairs and across the empty dance floor to the pool tables.

As the evening wore on, I found myself relaxing around my friends, happy there wasn't any apparent backlash from Bianca's lies. I was having trouble concentrating whenever I got a glimpse of her. Worse, this was the first time I'd seen her and some of the other ladies make their way to the dance floor. As the bar got busier, I noticed more and more men approaching looking to dance with her but she never left her friends.

"Bianca looks great, Schicker. All that racquetball is paying off." The unknown twenty-something man said, his eyes lighting up as he spoke of the woman he'd just passed on the dance floor. He put his new beer down on the edge of the pool table, prompting Greg to chastise him.

"Hey, dumbass, that's what the bar rail is for." Greg pointed to the ledge that bordered the entirety of the pool table area.

"Charlie, can you believe this dumbass?" He motioned to the stranger with his head.

I was about to answer when Greg interrupted, "Do you know Josh?"

"No," I started to walk over and shake his hand when Greg continued. "Josh works over in Bianca's building."

"Oh, nice to meet you, man," I instead chose to throw him a chin jut.

"What's up?" He took a swig of beer and continued, "So how often do you guys play?"

I was about to answer when I realized he wasn't talking to me. I noticed he kept his focus on Bianca and her friends. I looked over at the group but really I was only watching her. Just then, the DJ spun a new record, the ladies giggled and seemed to really get into the song.

"We've been playing twice a week for a few weeks now," Greg smiled proudly as he watched Bianca and the others. "She's amazing," he took a sip of Scotch and savored it. "Charlie here is a member of the club, too. He was my regular partner until Bianca and I started playing. She's actually quite good."

"She's good with angles," I thought to myself.

We continued watching the women dancing, completely ignoring our game. As the catchy Bobby Brown tune continued, I noticed the women, most of them having removed their shoes, eventually fell into the "Electric Slide". When Bianca turned toward us and saw us all watching her, she seemed to like the attention. She smiled then did the next required turn with the rest of the group. I decided it was best to continue with the game and did what I could to keep from thinking about her.

Sometime later Greg excused himself, leaving Josh and I alone at the pool table.

"I can't believe Bianca can be so cool and so fucked up." He chugged the remainder of his beer and let it fall a little too hard on the bar rail. "I mean, I'd totally fuck her but not if I could lose my job. You know?" He looked around for the waitress. "I just can't believe she'd try to fuck you over like that. You seem like a cool guy."

That's all it took. Just as I saw Greg coming back down the stairs, I excused myself and walked toward him. "I'll be right back," I grunted as I passed him then took the stairs two at a time. I was wondering what I was going to say or how I'd be able to say it in front of an audience but as luck would have it, Bianca was on her way out the front door.

I followed her into the lobby and grabbed her by the arm, "I have to talk to you," was all I said. She asked where we were going and asked me to let go of her but I didn't comply. I didn't say a word. I couldn't. At that point, I still wasn't sure what I was going to say. We walked to the furthest corner of the parking lot where a shuttle bus was parked in a well-lit corner. As we rounded the bumper, she asked, "What's the problem?" The school-girl innocence in her face infuriated me and I pushed her into the cold steel of the bus. "Why are you doing this?" I shouted at her.

As she struggled against me, I pinned her hands with mine. I felt the same electricity I felt earlier in the evening and I kissed her mouth. I soon found us kissing passionately, her tongue mingling with mine, moving together like a well-choreographed tango. It was like the calls and texts, the lies, and Jeff Syddall didn't matter. In that moment, she was the Bianca I knew.

She suddenly pushed me away and as she was turning to leave, she tripped over her feet and hit the side of the bus.

"Leave me the fuck alone!" She yelled at me, her eyes glazed with tears. "Don't think I can't hurt you."

I stood there stunned at what I'd done, fearing how it was going to look. When Bianca tripped, she'd hit her face causing her nose to bleed. I knew she'd previously made an accusation against me and now with this kind of physical evidence people might actually believe her. How would I be able to explain to my friends that I dragged her outside and she ended up with a bloody nose? Something told me most of them might not be my friends much longer. I watched her stumbling away then hung my head and wondered what had gone so wrong.

Bianca was the most amazing woman I'd ever met and cause of the most improbable humiliation I'd ever felt.

* * *

A couple days of unplanned vacation turned into a week. I just couldn't bring myself to face the people at work that I knew were there that night. And after seeing the look on Schicker's face when I last saw him in the lobby of the Westin, I knew it was best to avoid him as long as possible.

When I got back to the office, I heard mumbling about Ty getting engaged and the possibility of a change in our holiday schedule but I didn't perceive any disapproving looks or whispers from anyone. Apparently the time away had been the best and possibly only thing I could have done to mitigate my disgrace.

Lunch came and went without an invitation from my regular group. I knew Schicker was in Costa Rica but I saw the rest of my lunch posse crossing the parking lot and entering the building from the South entrance, the one visible from my office.

I had barely taken a few bites from the sandwich I'd bought in the cafeteria and thought it wasn't the worst thing in the world that I'd worked through lunch. I certainly had enough to do to keep me busy. Not the least of which was keeping up with Greg's stuff since he was in San Jose on what was supposed to be my project. I decided to work well into the evening and realized after 11 hours in the office, I hadn't gotten one pop-in or ping in chat from anyone. Was it possible they didn't know I was back in the office? Or was it possible they just didn't care?

By Thursday, I knew it wasn't an oversight. This was deliberate.

In the kitchen, people were polite but seemed to stop talking as soon as I entered the room. People spoke in whispers as they passed by my office and it was like all of a sudden I was "the new guy" even though I'd known most of these people for years. Clearly, people were staying away from me. I guess that's why I was startled when Ty knocked on my door the next morning.

"What's up, Charlie?" He was holding a travel mug of coffee in one hand and leaning against the door frame, "You got a minute?"

"Sure," I said swiveling around in my chair away from my computer and facing him, "what's up?"

He strolled into my office and took a seat. He crossed his legs and held the stainless steel travel mug on his knee, holding it with one hand, drumming his fingers on the arm of the chair with his free hand. Clearly, he was uncomfortable.

I decided to break the awkward pause, "I hear you and Lynn are getting engaged. Congratulations." I tried to smile at him even though my nerves were making a smile physically impossible.

He let out an audible sigh and then smiled, "Yeah, she's great. I'm a lucky guy," he didn't make eye contact. "We're having a party Saturday night."

"Yeah, I heard something about that," I didn't tell him that I was thinking of any reason not to go. "I'm sure that'll be a great time." I swallowed the nervousness that was climbing up my throat.

He took a tentative sip of his coffee and shifted in his seat, "Charlie, I didn't invite you to the party." He took another sip of his coffee and finally looked at me.

There was a flood of emotion that washed over me and my face must have shown it. Ty looked away and mumbled something under his breath. I could feel heat stinging my eyes and I concentrated on controlling my breathing, I had to regain control of my emotions. The shame spiral I was on was certain to cause me significant embarrassment.

"I'm sorry," he sighed, "I'm not trying to hurt your feelings, man." He sat forward in his chair and put the coffee down on the edge of my desk. "I love Lynn and this thing with you and her friend has really put me in a tough spot. I mean, she didn't tell me not to invite you, it was my decision. But Lynn's a good woman, I don't want anyone or anything to ruin this night for us."

There was the embarrassment again.

"I understand," I looked to the hallway and wondered if I should have closed the door. "I don't want to ruin anything for you either."

"Aw, man, I don't mean it like that. I don't think you'd do anything intentional."

I shook my head, "Never."

"Well, I'm sure you've noticed some people have been a little quiet around here and that's probably because of the party. I kinda had to make it known that I wasn't inviting you because I didn't want anyone to tell you about it." He looked around, "I know I should have talked to you sooner but I proposed to Lynn the night that whole thing went down with you and Bianca in the parking lot. I'm actually surprised you're here. I thought you were gonna be in Costa Rica this week."

"Schicker went," I mumbled.

"Yeah," he sighed again, "well, anyway..." his voice trailed off.

"I'm happy for you guys. You're a great couple."

Another awkward few moments of silence as Ty sat back in his seat and sipped his coffee. I could tell he was just waiting for the right moment to leave.

I finally grabbed my empty coffee mug and showed it to him, "I'm gonna go find some coffee."

"Yeah, sure." He practically jumped out of his chair, "I should get going anyway."

I began following him out of my office when he quickly turned around, "You wanna come over Sunday? We could have a couple beers and watch the game." He must have read the hesitation on my face and quickly commented, "Lynn's gonna be in Tyson's Corner all day."

"Yeah. Let's do it," I patted him on the back as we walked out of my office.

Not that there would ever be a good time to have the kind of blow out I had with Bianca but I had no idea it was one of the most important nights of my friend's life. At least now I knew why people were avoiding me.

I arrived at Ty's townhouse in Germantown and parked in one of the few visitor spots a half-block away. He opened the door before I even got up the stairs. With a beer in his hand, he smiled, "C'mon man, we're gonna miss the opening kickoff."

I had only been to his house a few times but I could tell the difference from when he was a bachelor and now that a woman was in his life. His home was tastefully decorated, he had an excellent eye for style and fashion but I could definitely tell by the pleasant smell of lemongrass that subtly wafted from room-to-room that a woman spent a lot of time here.

We walked through the living room to the island in the center of the kitchen. There was a miniature metal wash bucket partially filled with ice water and a variety of imported bottles of beer. Right next to it sat a platter with sandwiches and several small bowls of potato chips and pretzels. There was so much food and beer, I wondered if he'd invited anyone else.

"I didn't know what you like so I just got a few different kinds of whatever. None of them have cheese though, I remembered that much," he waved his hand in the direction of the food. "Some stuff is left over from last night," he looked around the kitchen, found the bottle opener and placed it on the island next to the beer. "Help yourself."

I put a plate together and grabbed a beer. As I walked from the kitchen to the great room, I noticed a pile of still-wrapped presents along the wall. I figured they'd gotten them last night and hadn't yet had the time to open them.

"So Lynn's out dress shopping or something?" I asked as I got to my seat on the long, chocolate brown sofa.

"No. She's gonna do that when Bianca gets back from Costa Rica." He took a huge bite of his turkey hoagie but immediately stopped chewing and looked at me. Speaking with his mouth full of food, "You knew she went with Schicker, right?"

I felt like I'd gotten punched in the gut. My stomach was suddenly in my throat and the smell of the sandwich on the plate in front of me and the previously pleasant smell of lemongrass were making me nauseous.

"Actually, no. I guess I'm kinda outta the loop," I put my plate on my lap and forced myself to take a bite.

I couldn't tell you what game was on. Was it the Redskins or the Ravens? I have no idea. This wasn't about the game, it was about my friend. This was about trying to make things right with him. And as I tried to listen intently about player statistics and what it all meant to his fantasy football standing, I couldn't help thinking about Greg and Bianca together.

I did manage to get through my sandwich but by the time I went to take a second drink of my beer, it was warm and I didn't have the courage to get a cold one. I sat in the far corner of the sofa and picked at the label on the beer bottle when I heard Ty raise his voice, "Charlie, you alright?"

I snapped out of my dense thoughts, "Yeah, man. I'm good. This is great. The sandwich was really good. Where did you get it?"

"Safeway," he said with a half-hearted laugh. "Really? C'mon man, what's up?"

I continued picking at the label and didn't look up at him. I didn't know what to say. I finally put the bottle down on the lapis coaster on the end table next to me and turned on the cushion to face him. I rested my left foot on my right knee and put my elbow on the back of the sofa.

Ty sat forward in his chair, put his empty beer bottle on the coffee table in front of us and waited for me to speak.

"I just feel like shit," I slapped my thigh, "I feel like shit and I just don't know how to make things right." A humble admission for me.

"With Bianca?" Ty got up, "You want another beer? That one's probably warm," he walked into the kitchen and quickly returned with two more beers without even waiting for my answer.

I nodded and took the sweating bottle from his hand, careful not to drop it, "With everyone, I guess."

"You and I are cool, Charlie. Alright? But I'm not gonna lie, Lynn does have a serious problem with you. And I'm not exactly sure what happened or why. But whatever it was with you and Bianca, she didn't deserve that shit. And to be honest, if you were anyone else, you wouldn't be sitting on my couch right now. I've been knowing you a long time, Diaz," he took a long swig of his beer, "I'm not gonna get in your business but if I may give you some advice?"

"Sure," I took a drink and braced myself.

He put his beer down, "Whatever it is that's caused you to be such a fucking mess over this, you need to handle it before you lose more than a woman."

I nodded, "I'm so embarrassed, man. You have no idea." I shook my head the more I thought about it.

"Embarrassed? You should be *ashamed* of what you did to that girl."

"I am," I said contritely.

"Don't let the shame stop you from doing the right thing, man," he picked up his beer and gestured with it. "You have some work to do on you. Then get this thing right."

"She just made me so mad. I mean, fuck. All the hang up calls and cryptic text messages. It was like, leave me alone already. And I don't know, when I saw her that night, she was acting like nothing happened and I just – I don't know." I was now quickly slugging down my beer.

"Charlie, is she crazy?" He eyed me intently waiting for my answer.

"I don't think she's crazy."

"Is she stupid?" I could see by the look on his face I'd have to answer this question carefully.

"No." I shook my head and put my now empty bottle down on a different coaster, "She's not stupid at all."

"So let me ask you this, if she's calling and texting from her phone, doesn't she know you can see the caller ID?"

We sat there in silence as Ty finished his beer and was about to get another round when we heard keys in the door. My heart pounded in my chest as Lynn walked in with an armful of bridal magazines.

She nodded at me and walked over to her fiancé. They kissed briefly, Ty keeping one eye on me as if to ask me to leave. I tried to take my plate and bottles to the kitchen but my friend quickly dismissed my effort, "I'll get it," he said with a tight smile.

I gave them both a quick "thank you" and rushed out the door.

As I drove Interstate 270 to my side of the Capital Beltway, his words echoed in my mind.

Is Bianca crazy?

She's not stupid.

Why would she do this?

Before I even had a chance to get coffee, Greg was at my office door with a quick rap on the door frame, "You got a minute?"

"Did you have a nice trip?" I asked looking around, wondering why he'd closed the door.

"We need to talk," he said standing with his back against the door.

I motioned to the sofa on the far wall and invited him to sit down, "OK."

Greg told me about the lies. He told me about his confession to Bianca. And, he told me a few things I never expected to hear. I sat behind my desk listening, completely unable to react to what he was saying.

"Why?" It was all I could manage.

Greg ran his fingers through his hair, "I don't know."

"What about all the phone calls? The texts?"

"In the beginning that was her..."

I exhaled deeply, "*In the beginning?*"

Greg looked me straight in the eyes, not daring to blink, "Sometimes we'd be out, her phone was right there. I'd let it go just long enough that the caller ID would – "

"You're fucking sinister, man," I stood up and began to pace the suddenly very tiny office.

"I'll never be able to make this up to her. Or you." Greg put his elbows on his knees and hung his head. "I tried to explain everything to her but she won't listen. She still doesn't know everything."

"You tell me and *I'll* tell her," I clenched my teeth and I tried hard not raise my voice.

"Candace," Greg said still not looking at me.

"Candace?" I squeezed my eyes closed and threw my head back.

"Candace liked you and would do anything to show you. So when I told her, she jumped at the chance to – "

"To what?" Now I was shouting.

He looked around as if the closed door wasn't enough to prevent people from hearing my raised voice, "I told her I was worried."

"Worried about what?" I shouted again and then tried to compose myself.

"Worried she might try to get you fired or something."

"What?"

"Like that deal with her English teacher. She ruined that man's life. I heard he got arrested and everything. You think he could ever teach again after that?"

"English teacher? What the fuck are you talking about?"

"I told you about that. She got him fired from his job – "

"Did you make that up, too? Fucking asshole." I started to throw a punch at the door then pulled it from the air. I wanted to put my fist through the wall, I wanted to put my fist in his face but all I could do was stand there in anger and astonishment, and hope he'd eventually get to the part where none of this happened.

"No, that part is actually true."

"And what the fuck has that got to do with me?" I gripped the chair in front of me, seeing the knuckles on my hands turning white against the black fabric. "All this time, you were making it look as though she was obsessed with me?" I walked back to my desk keeping a wide berth, "Why?"

"I really don't know." Greg turned his face away from me.

"Yeah, you do. You know full fucking well." I walked to my office door and swung it open with controlled anger, "You never forgave me for that whole thing with Karen."

Greg got up to walk out but stood his ground for another moment, "I'm sorry."

"Lemme ask you this," I partially closed the door, keeping my fingers wrapped around the handle, "I mean, I know why you wanted to hurt me but why did you wanna hurt her?"

"Honestly? Maybe because I couldn't believe another woman I wanted actually wanted you." He walked past me with a huff and stopped in the threshold, "I think she really cares about you, Charlie. She didn't deserve what I did to her."

"But I did," now it was my turn to hang my head.

"Can we get past this?" He asked in a quiet, humble tone.

I looked up at him. It was like looking into the eyes of a stranger, "I don't know. But I hope she and I can."

"Me, too," he slapped my chest and walked out.

I sat at my desk for what felt like an eternity evaluating my level of shame and embarrassment over the situation. Now that I could better understand why I reacted the way I did, I wondered if I would ever be able to explain it to her. Even after the lies Greg told, was what I had done worse?

Unequivocally, yes.

Lynn shook her head the minute she saw me walk into the office suite, "No, no, no. No way. I woulda thought you'd have enough sense not to come here." She rose from her chair, "I will tolerate you because the man I love, for some reason, thinks you're worth a damn but you and I both know if I had my choice, I'd never see your punk ass again. Now, I suggest you turn around and walk right out that door you just came in before shit gets real in here." She walked around her desk as she spoke, "you've done enough." She was angrier than I'd ever seen her.

"I've been an asshole, I have a lot of explaining to do, I know. Can't I just talk to her?"

"No fucking way."

"Seriously. I think once I explain everything – "

"You are not serious," arms folded, she shook her head, "there's no way you could ever explain away what you've done to that girl."

"I know how this must sound but I've really gotta talk to her," I pressed her but didn't move from where I stood. "Can you please just tell her I'm here?"

She let out a fake laugh, "No. I can't."

"Is she here?" I asked, realizing we were standing in front of her empty desk.

"Nope."

"Where is she?" I looked around for evidence that she was there. Perhaps a half-drank cup of coffee, a sweater on the back of her chair, anything.

"Mexico," her tone was sarcastically pleasant.

"Like on vacation?"

Lynn explained Bianca was in the midst of a career change that would not only take her from her current position with the nuclear engineering firm but most likely from D.C. also.

"It's a job interview, asshole," she told me reluctantly.

"She's gonna move to Mexico?" I spoke much louder than I'd intended and caught the attention of one of the engineers walking out of the kitchen. He strode over and asked if everything was alright.

"Hey, Tommy. Everything's fine," Lynn tried to sound convincing.

"Are you Tommy Payton? I've heard a lot about you. Charlie Diaz." I held out my hand to shake his, "Bianca told me – "

"You need to leave," he said and briskly showed me out.

"Hold on, I need to talk to Lynn." I said trying to break free from his surprisingly strong grip around my right bicep, "Lynn, please just listen."

She made a mocking waving gesture and turned to walk back to her desk.

Tommy not only escorted me out of their office suite but walked me down the stairs and out the front of the building.

The air was thin and cold, "This woman went to El Salvador alone because of you. What the hell is wrong with you?"

"Excuse me, Sir?" I turned to face him as he huddled in the corner and lit a cigarette.

"She went to El Salvador, a third-world country, alone because you're a fucking coward," he took a long contented drag from his cigarette.

"Mr. Payton, let me just say something here, I know I've made a lot of mistakes where Bianca is concerned but – "

"It's Doctor Payton," he barked.

I looked around to make sure we had privacy in the front of the busy bank building. "Dr. Payton, like I was telling Lynn, I've just gotta get the chance to talk to her. I know it won't make up for everything but if I had a chance to at least explain some – "

"What if no one cares what you have to say? What then?" His pale blue eyes twinkled with contempt.

"I honestly don't know."

"Well, you might wanna think about that," he took another deep drag from the cigarette and promptly blew smoke out of his nose.

"I have."

"So are you gonna explain why couldn't you just be a decent person and tell her everything before you went 3,000 miles away?"

I instinctively started to apologize when I realized I had no idea what he was talking about, "Wait. What?"

"I'm talking about how you fucked around with her life and like a coward, didn't come clean until you had her where you wanted her. What did you expect her to do? Be grateful that you finally told the truth?" He shook his head, "And just before the holidays? Nice touch, asshole." His Boston accent was suddenly audible.

"I don't understand."

"A man with some balls would've told her about the lies here," he pointed to the ground with the hand that was holding the cigarette.

"Dr. Payton, I have no idea what you're talking about."

He looked at me blankly, "Costa Rica? Fucking with her life. Lying. These things don't sound familiar?"

"She went to Costa Rica with Greg Schicker. I'm Charlie Diaz."

Tommy's head flipped up and his once angry eyes became enraged. He ditched his cigarette and stomped on it. "So you're the guy that gave her the black eye?" He whipped around and started to walk back inside, "Lynn's right, you need to go."

"Wait," I followed him.

We stood in the noisy lobby of the bank building and stared at each other. Tommy seemed to be searching my face for something.

"We've both been lied to, Sir. We've both been lied to from the very beginning." I did the best I could in that situation to tell him as much information as quickly as possible. At certain times of my rapid fire explanation I could see him become frustrated with me but he indulged me with his patience and silence for as long as he could.

"So what do you want?" He shrugged and gave a languid look at the door to the stairwell.

"Honestly? I don't know."

And that was the truth.

"All I can say is that trip changed her," he sighed, "you changed her." I watched as he bounded up the stairs, taking them two at a time and disappeared.

I knew I was going to have to get to her a different way.

After hours of brainstorming, I knew. As much as I hated to do it, I was going to have to ask Schicker for his help. I stopped by his office and asked if I could come in. His eyes lit up as he invited me to sit down. "It's not what you think," I said taking a seat, "I need your help."

"What?" His suddenly stern tone told me this wasn't going to be easy.

"I need you to help me get in touch with Bianca's friend, Dee Dee."

"What?" He shook his head, "No way, man," he got up and closed the door. "I'm sorry," he said returning to his desk, "I can't do that."

"You owe me. You owe us both."

"No can do," he clasped his hands on his desk. "Just stop by her office," his dismissive tone was infuriating.

"She's not there and Lynn won't help. And I don't have the audacity to ask Ty."

"Well, I'm sorry. I can't help you. I made a promise and I'm sticking to it."

I waited a few days before approaching Greg again, this time in the parking lot of our office. He was more adamant and I was more insistent, "Greg, I'm serious. What I did was wrong but what you did was worse because you hurt a completely innocent person in the process of trying to settle a score with me. She didn't deserve this and you know it."

"I can't," he continued to his car. "I'm not going to continue to embarrass myself over this. And neither should you."

All I could do was stand there and watch him drive away. I thought for a moment. Who would be willing to give me a chance? Who could I convince that I was sorry? There was only one person I could think of and it was a long shot. I'd never met her but I'd been to her house once.

Her name was Elle.

I rang the doorbell and rehearsed what I'd say to Elle to convince her to tell me how I could get in touch with Bianca. It had been a few weeks since my failed attempt to talk to her at her office. Ty told me she resigned to take the position with the international sales group of a company based out of Germany and was doing a lot of traveling in her new position. She never answered any of my calls or emails but I thought if I could at least see her and apologize, we might be able to get over the past year of pain we'd caused each other, wittingly and unwittingly.

Elle called from somewhere inside the house, "Just come on in. Kitty is locked up in the bedroom." I cautiously walked into the house hoping not to scare her when she realized I wasn't who she was expecting.

The spunky, petite woman talked 100 miles an hour about counter-tops before she even saw me, then surmised, "You're not the granite guy are you?" I guess she could tell by how I was dressed or maybe because I didn't have any sample cases.

"No. Actually, I'm here to talk to you about Bianca."

"What do you want?" Her demeanor suddenly changed and she grabbed a cordless phone as she flew through the living room and pushed me out the front door, "Bianca isn't home."

"I know," I tried hard to appear as non-threatening as possible. "I'm Charlie Diaz. I – "

"You need to leave," she yelled and pushed my chest with one hand beginning to dial 9-1-1 with the other.

"Wait," I didn't put up any physical resistance but pleaded with her to listen.

Once we were outside she picked up little stones from her front yard landscaping and began throwing them at my car, "Get the fuck out of here." Even though she was getting dangerously close to marring the paint on my car, I didn't want to leave. I stepped in front of the stones she hurled, each one stinging. She picked up a second handful and started throwing harder. I suddenly wished I'd left my coat on.

"I know I deserve this but she deserves an explanation of everything. Please."

"You don't deserve shit, Charlie. Least of all a nice girl like her," she started throwing the small white stones two and three at a time. "Now go or I'll call the cops," she picked up another handful of rocks.

"I said *she* deserves it, not me. Can you please just hear me out?"

"OK, *you* start talking and *I'll* start throwing rocks when you piss me off."

I explained as quickly as I could. Schicker's lies and how everything precipitated from that. My details were specific but chronologically out of order as I struggled to get as much information as I could to the last person that could help me.

She let the rocks fall from her hands back into the flower bed where she'd picked them up. She clapped her hands together and brushed the dirt from her hands. "It's cold. I gotta go inside."

"Please." I took a couple of steps toward her but then stopped when she looked up and glared at me, "Maybe you could just tell me when I can come by and see her?"

"I really don't know what you expect me to do," she leaned against the front door, her hand on the knob.

"I just want her to have the truth and find out what she wants to do." I rubbed my hands together and blew on them to warm them, "I'll respect her decision, whatever it is."

"She's on a 20-day swing through deep South America right now," she looked around as though she was telling me something I wasn't supposed to know. "She said when she gets back she's gonna start looking at moving to either Miami or Dallas."

"Miami or Dallas?"

"Two of the main gateways for South America. She travels a lot for her new job. She thought about Atlanta but immediately ruled it out."

"Schicker's from Atlanta," I thought to myself, sure that was a factor in her decision. "Well, she hasn't moved yet, right? When do you think I'd have the best chance to catch her?"

"You think it's going to change anything?"

"I don't know. But at the very least, I have to try."

"Why?" She asked skeptically.

"Because I wanna know her. And I want her to know me. And I haven't wanted that from a woman in a very long time."

"What if you're too late?"

"I'll be OK with that. But until I get a chance to explain to her, I don't think I can be OK and quite honestly, I don't think she will be either."

"So, what do you wanna do?"

"I wanna talk to her. I wanna tell her everything." I leaned against the wood rail lining the flower bed, and put my right hand over my heart, "Elle, I've been trying for weeks to find a way to get in touch with her. I just want a chance. We never even had a chance."

Elle opened the door and motioned me over. She walked through the living room and disappeared behind a wall that blocked the living room from the dining room then quickly came back, flipping through a spiral notebook. She stopped on a blank page and began writing.

She looked up at me, "Do you have a passport?"

I sat in the lobby of the Hilton on the Wharf and wondered if I had done the right thing. Elle had written down a list of cities and dates, and told me as soon as I made a choice, she'd give me the hotel information. She wouldn't tell me when Bianca would be back in Maryland or for how long, only that once she made it back stateside, she'd be spending time in both Miami and Dallas, deciding where she wanted to live.

I considered the dozen or so cities and determined this was really the only option I had because it was the only place where she'd be longer than a couple of days. The worst possible scenario was missing her because of a flight delay.

This was the place. Today was the day.

"Mr. Diaz, do you need help to your room?" The bell captain asked in a strong Spanish accent.

"No. Thank you, I'm just waiting for someone."

"Very good, Sir," he said returning to his post.

I ventured outside and looked at the sparkling waters of the wharf. The 14-hour plane ride had sapped most of my energy, stretching my legs and getting some fresh air was doing me good. I hated flying and the feeling of jetlag but the thought she'd be there soon made me feel better. I had thought about checking in and leaving a message for her but worried she might simply leave as soon as she knew I was there. I had no choice but to wait.

My heart skipped a beat when I saw her. She was wearing stylish black slacks and a fitted, pinstriped shirt. Her smooth dark brown hair, now quite a big longer, was pulled back into a loose pony tail. She pulled a large wheeled bag behind her as she strode up to the front desk. I smiled to myself, a strange sense of pride just knowing her.

The whole flight down I rehearsed what I'd say and now being there, I had no idea how to start. But I'd come this far and needed to seize the opportunity.

As she crossed the expanse of the lobby to the elevators, she noticed me. Her confident smile instantly left her face and was replaced by a blush of anger.

I slung my weekender over my shoulder and approached her. She stopped walking and hung her head.

"What are you doing here?" She said shifting her weight to one foot and crossing her arms around herself.

I strained to get closer without intimidating her, "I came here to see you."

"What do you want?" Her eyes avoided mine as she looked past me and examined the impressive, bustling lobby.

"You're not surprised to see me," I took a deep breath. "Elle called you."

She nodded, still avoiding eye contact.

"I had to talk to you."

"So talk," she shifted her weight to the opposite foot in a gesture of frustration.

"I don't know where to start."

"OK, well enjoy Buenos Aires," she unfolded her arms and started to walk away.

"Wait," I said stepping in front of her.

"I'm tired. I've had a long day."

"Can I buy you dinner or something so we can talk?"

"No," she stepped around me and started again toward the elevators.

"Bianca, I flew all this way – "

She spun around on her heels and walked up to me, "You flying all this way means fuck all. The time for you to do the right thing was when Schicker gave you all that bullshit. You chose to believe the worst in me." I could see the anger in her eyes, like the strike of a match, a sudden ignition of ire, she slightly squinted, "It would have taken answering just one of my emails or just one of my phone calls to straighten things out." She leaned in, "Now you know that feeling."

I felt a lump of emotion in my chest, truth and shame sucking the air from my lungs.

"By the way, I hope you're flying business class, you look like shit."

"Wait," I mustered all the strength I could. After weeks of thinking about this moment, it was here and I had to do it.

"What?" She snapped at me, drawing the attention of two young Argentine men in suits that were standing nearby.

"I'm not here to make excuses."

She continued walking past me, "Just go home, Charlie. Go home and move on. I have."

And there it was.

"Just tell me one thing," I said loud enough for her to hear me over the increasingly noisy expanse of the grand foyer. She continued walking away but I could see the hesitation in her gait, "If Schicker hadn't…" I didn't know how to say it.

She stopped. I wasn't sure if I should close the gap so I stood my ground and waited. She slowly turned around, dropping her head to one side, "What kind of question is that?"

"You felt it. I know you did. That night in the parking lot – "

"Which time?" The sarcasm in her voice stung.

"The first night we met. I know you felt it. That's why you kept reaching out to me because you knew I felt it, too. So, I'm here.

197

I'm here right now. Almost a year after that one date we had, I flew 14 hours to get to see you again because you're worth it. I'm right here, right now telling you I want to know you. And I know you're afraid."

"Of you?" Her eyes seared mine but I didn't look away.

"Of everyone."

"Because you're every man I've ever been involved with Charlie. I don't even have relationships, I have some kind of fucking syndrome," her voice was tight with emotion.

"I'm sorry for everything I did but you have to know that's not the real me. Schicker played us both. And I was so scared because of what had happened with Karen – "

"I'm not a gold-digging whore from Arkansas," she said walking away.

She frantically pressed the "up" arrow and looked up to watch the floor numbers on the digital display above the elevator doors.

I slowly approached the arriving elevator car, careful to let her know I wasn't going to join her, "I'm sorry Bianca. And if you think you could ever begin to forgive me..." I didn't know how to finish that thought either.

She gripped the handle of her luggage with both hands, staring at the elevator floor and did nothing to stop the doors from closing.

I saw my hotel room for the first time almost five hours after arriving. I threw my bag on one of the two double beds in the room and looked around, "Now what?"

I lie cross-wise on the bed, picked my glasses off of my nose and rubbed my aching eyes. I wasn't sure if I'd over-estimated myself or under-estimated her. Even though I'd seen it, I hadn't considered her anger. I thought coming all the way to Argentina she would certainly know how sorry I was. I closed my eyes and wondered if I'd ever be able to do anything to earn her forgiveness.

* * *

I awoke a few hours later, my head pounding from hunger and jetlag. I looked at my watch and realized I didn't know if Buenos Aires was on D.C. time. I began searching for a clock and figured it had been almost an entire day since I'd had anything to eat.

I went to the bathroom to splash water on my face. I looked at my reflection and thought about what Bianca had said, "...you look like shit." She was right. I decided to take a shower before going to find my next meal.

I thought it was a sign when I spotted her sitting at a table in the nearly empty hotel bar. She'd changed clothes, now wearing a white knit top, her long hair now loose but still wavy from the pony tail she wore earlier. She had a half-empty rock glass in front of her and twirled the skinny red straw in between her thumb and forefinger. She rested her elbow on the table in front of her, her hand on her neck, as if her own touch was reassuring her. I wasn't sure what I would do but I knew I was going to do something. I could hear the television in the corner, some kind of sports coverage, otherwise the bar was quiet. As I got closer, she didn't look up but I saw the expression on her face change. It was as if she felt my presence.

Adrenaline kicked in and I tried to be charming, "Excuse me, Miss. I noticed you were alone. Can I join you for a drink?"

She forced a smile on her face and looked up at me, "I'm waiting for someone." I held her gaze when she suddenly lit up. In that moment, I saw the Bianca I knew that one perfect day back in D.C.

"Sorry to keep you waiting," I heard him say.

He walked around me and pulled out her chair. She stood up and they locked in an embrace. I could see her whole body melt in his arms. I couldn't help the jealousy that suddenly surged inside of me.

Never letting go of her waist, the blonde man turned his attention to me, "Who's your friend?" He flaunted a wide, white smile.

"Charlie Diaz," I answered quickly, trying to chase the nerves from my body as I offered a slightly trembling hand.

I could tell by the excessive pressure of his handshake, he knew who I was. Bianca turned her body to face me, his left arm still wrapped around her. She beamed with a pride I'd never seen as he introduced himself.

"Good to meet you, I'm Jeff Syddall."

Read on for the prologue to
ENGLISH 101

Prequel to "The Charlie Diaz Syndrome"

PROLOGUE

Jon stood next to his desk reading his paper on "Antigone", fumbling over words as jocks tend to do. He's pretty but not very articulate and really it isn't his fault. Nothing could hold my interest in this class. There's a knock on the door, turning everyone's attention to find my Administrator, Mr. Gerardi, a burly man with dark hair and thick moustache.

He hung on the door jamb, "Bianca, I need you for a minute."

Mr. Syddall stood up and got to threshold of the door as I crossed the room and walked past him into the hall. There stood a Palatine Police Officer, a 30-something man with a buzz cut, holding a set of handcuffs.

He asks me to verify my name and date of birth. Yes. I am one of the few 18 year old incoming Seniors at Palatine High School. Because my Mom forgot to enroll me in school the year she should have, I am older than most of the kids in my class. But it hasn't always been this way. Although I am a Senior in high school, I've already attended college and am classified as "gifted" with a measured IQ of 160. I'm only in *English 101* for the same reason I'm in pre-algebra – I need the credit hours in the respective disciplines so I can graduate. I need to get out of this fucking place.

Officer Buzz Cut tells me to turn around and put my hands behind my back and the sound of his two-way radio going off draws students to the doorway just in time to see the silver cuffs tighten around my wrists.

"Do you have to hand cuff her?" Mr. Syddall says with an ache in his voice.

"It's for her protection and mine. And it's policy, Sir."

"My protection? You're the one with the gun," I snap at him.

"Stay out of this Stephen," Mr. Gerardi says in a stern voice. He's the only one I know that calls Jeff by his first name and not his prefer- ence, which is his middle name. I figure it's a power move and a way for Mr. Gerardi to remind him he is the boss. "And Bianca, you keep quiet."

I wince as the officer tightens the cuff around my left wrist which is still not entirely healed, prompting another plea from Mr. Syddall, "Do you have to cuff her behind her back?"

And just as Mr. Gerardi is about to reprimand Jeff again, it's my turn to protest.

"This is fucking bullshit. I have no idea what Mrs. Kelly is up to now but I'm telling you, I didn't do anything." I feel the anger like a knife twisting in my heart, "Fuck her and her son." I'm looking directly at my friend, Jon, who's now standing in the hallway along with a few other students and watching the action up close.

I know he's friends with Mike or was until he became friends with me Junior year. Our friendship had actually cost him a lot and I always had some regret that he took a stand for me. It was only through one fortuitous afternoon stuck in the school elevator that we became friends. If not for us both having a broken leg, for different reasons of course, we wouldn't have even been in that elevator. But he was now one of my dearest friends. He's a nice boy from a good family so I make sure to keep my distance. I'd already learned my lesson with Mike Kelly that even though I was a good girl, I was from "the wrong side of the tracks" and I wasn't the kind of girl his Mother would want for him. Sweet, Jon.

The more I pushed him away, the more he wanted to be around me. *Why do we always want the things we shouldn't have?*

"That's enough," Mr. Gerardi barks at me, "no need for that language."

"Mr. Gerardi, I haven't done anything. This is just some more bullshit from the Kelly's and yeah I'd love to burn down their – "

The Officer is reading me the Mirandas and both Mr. Syddall and Mr. Gerardi tell me to stop talking.

"Bianca, stop," Jeff says just as the Officer asks if I understand my rights.

"Of course I understand them. And I understand this is bullshit. I have no idea how Mrs. Kelly got you to come arrest me but you're – "

"What are the charges, Officer?" Jon asks politely, looking just about as innocent as a baby deer.

"Everyone, get back in class," Mr. Syddall says as the Officer turns me around and walks me to the stairwell with Mr. Gerardi in tow.

"Yeah, that's a good question. It would be nice to know what that bitch accused me of now." We're taking the stairs from the 3rd floor English wing down to the main floor and my Administrator once again tells me to keep quiet.

"The warrant is for vandalism, destruction of property in excess of ten thousand dollars and leaving the scene of an accident."

All at once I see stars and I feel my legs go weak. I almost fall down but luckily the Officer has a firm grip on my right arm and keeps me from falling.

"Bianca, is there someone you want me to call? I know you probably don't want me to call your Mom but is there anyone else?"

I wanted to tell him that the only person to call already knew my predicament and would be at the Palatine Police Station as soon as possible but instead I asked him to call my emergency contact, "Dee Dee Donovan, she's my boss."

The Officer hits the long aluminum strike bar on one of the heavy red doors of my high school and leads me to a waiting squad car with another Officer leaning against the passenger side door of the cruiser. He opens the door to the backseat as we approach and I ask in a quiet voice if he can be careful with my wrist when he puts me in the car. He says nothing but is as careful as he probably can be but the pain still shoots up my arm and to the palm of my hand but it's nothing like the sickening pain in my stomach at that moment.

I wish I could say this was the most humiliating, frightening thing that ever happened to me at Palatine High School but I'd be lying.

www.ingramcontent.com/pod-product-compliance
Lightning Source LLC
Chambersburg PA
CBHW031313120626
46554CB00001BA/393